A Vampire's Chase

FATE'S CHRONICLES
BOOK FOUR

RHIANNON FUTCH

Ebook ISBN: 978-1-7341002-9-7

Print ISBN: 978-1-955749-25-1

Cover by sunsetrosebooks.com

Editing by V. Editing Services

Contents

One

FATE

THIS HAS BEEN the strangest day ever. I know who my birth parents are now, certainly never would have seen that coming. My grandmother is a completely abusive bitch and my mom is stuck visiting her half the fucking year but has to take someone with her to keep from being killed so grandma's un-named lover, usually called the Beast, can take over her body.

Now, now I am on my way upstairs to see my lover and my kidnapper to make sure he has been given a room and not a cell. Everyone seemed to have accepted that Charles is going to work with us, especially after Dad laid down the whammy that I could have Devon and Charles as my mates. All I would need to do is allow it for Charles, Devon and I have had the soul bond for multiple of my lifetimes already. But Charles, well, I feel the pull of the bond. Like a circuit trying to complete, stopped by a thin film of corrosion. The problem there is, well, Charles spent a long time killing me every time he found me. I mean, if anything were going to put a strain on a possible relationship murder is the thing, right?

However, it would seem that I am wildly fucked up because I don't know that I can turn away from him anymore than I could turn away from Devon. So here I am, heading up the stairs to find out how things are going. At the top of the stairs I look around, I don't see any open doors or lights to give me a clue where anyone is. Not really a surprise, most of us can see in the dark so lights become less than necessary for most things. I'll just check my bedroom first. I wouldn't mind having a nice long conversation with my Devon about how much I have missed him along with some concrete, physical actions to demonstrate. Those happy thoughts in mind I head for my bedroom. As I step through the door I see my Devon on the bed naked and looking like a gift. I walk over to the foot of the bed, "Think there might be room in that big bed for me?"

Devon smiles slow and says, "Having you in this bed is all I have been dreaming about, come join me sexy and let's forget the world for a while." The benefits of being a vampire are many but being able to leap onto the bed and land lightly over Devon is top of the benefits list right now. I lean down to kiss him lightly and find myself crushed to his chest, the kiss gone from zero to inferno the moment our lips touched. The clothing I had on disappears with a snap of my fingers. I am on fire and when I come up for air I realize the flames have covered my body, I sit up and look down at Devon, "Are these hurting you at all?"

He flexes his cock so it stands up away from his body and lodges itself between my hot folds, "The only thing hurting me right now is not being inside you."

I grin at him as I rock my hips just enough to gain him entrance. He sucks air through his teeth as the tip enters just a little. I hold still until he stops shaking with need. Then I take his hands and place them on my hips, whispering, "Hold on tight." He moans loudly as I impale myself on him a centimeter at a time. His hands are clamped on my hips as he shakes with the need to pound into me. I reach the base and for one glorious moment we are fused together.

Then I raise up and we start pounding into each other, hard and fast like the weeks I was gone were years apart. He slides one hand across my belly, bringing his thumb down to press my clit and the whole world explodes for me. I feel him start to cum with me and it sets off another set of waves inside me.

I collapse on top of him and he wraps his arms around me, "Oh sweet Goddess I am so glad you are home."

I chuckle, "That's how it is? You just want me for the amazing sex?"

He lifts me up so he can look into my eyes, "No, I want you because I don't feel complete without you. I feel like half my soul resides within you. It has never been just about sex."

"I know, I missed you too," I say as I sit up fully. "I suppose now is as good a time as any to ask what you did with Charles?"

He laughs, "I didn't lock him in the basement if that is what you are asking. Actually, he is in the room to the right of ours. Probably just about dead over there from listening to you moan on my dick. Or possibly entertaining himself watching the light show that happens when you cum now."

"What do you mean, light show?"

"I mean you lit the place up like the Fourth of July when you came. It was a little distracting. But all the curtains are open so if his curtains are open he is likely to have seen the light show. Hell, if his curtains weren't open he might have seen it. You and your blue flames... flared? Exploded?"

"Oh. I guess that's a thing now. And Charles probably heard everything we did just now. Well, I guess it had to happen eventually." I move off of him and onto the bed next to him, staying near because I still want to keep contact with him. "Now that I am not as distracted with thoughts of sex, you heard what my father said. The two of you are tied to me. If I let it happen Charles could be soul bound to me as well. What are your thoughts on that?"

Devon sits up and leans back against the pillows, opening his arms for me to join him. I scoot over and lean my back against him, snuggling into the circle of his arms.

"I don't know that I really like it. And maybe that is because he and I have been at odds for so long or maybe it is because you are mine and I don't want to share. Maybe I am just still pretty fucking mad at him for all the times he took you away from me. Maybe it is because you have been back for five minutes and I am still mad and frustrated about that."

I shift so I can look at him, "Devon, no one is going to take me away from you ever again. I am going to go to the Underworld and I am going to train and learn how to best use my power to defend us all. No one is going to take me away from my family ever again."

"I might need some time. To adjust. Or maybe just to be around you for more than a minute without out someone trying to kill you or take you from me. I can bear letting him around you for now and I will try to be polite. He and I may have to work out our own issues in the sparring room downstairs."

I laugh a little, "You guys going to beat each other up till you feel better?"

"We just might."

I hear Charles from the other room, "I'm ready when you are."

I throw my hands up over my face, "Oh my Goddess, you have been listening the whole time?"

Charles says, "Sweetheart, I couldn't do anything but listen when you started moaning. The light show wasn't just a light show. It was more like raw sex blasting through the walls. The entire rest of the neighborhood is probably having sex right now thanks to you."

"Oh jeez..."

Devon chuckles, "Don't worry, the neighborhood could use some livening up."

From the other side of the wall Charles says, "You did manage to find the most boring neighborhood in the entire city to live in."

Well, this should be interesting. I hope the house survives.

FATE

I WAKE up looking at the ceiling above me, letting it sink in that I am really home. I feel Devon's arms around me keeping me warm and cuddled up to him. I sigh in pleasure and he squeezes me a little.

I snuggle into him, "Morning."

"Morning it is. Glad to see you are finally awake. I thought you might sleep the day away."

"Mmmhmm, it isn't morning?"

"No, it is late afternoon. Even Charles has left his room room a little while ago. I stayed just to enjoy being here with you."

"I'm glad you stayed. I think I just didn't sleep as well with Pru in the same house. I was expending a lot of energy maintaining shields all over the place too. Home with you and the rest of the family I can finally relax."

"I like the way you say home with me and the rest of the family. Makes me feel all warm and fuzzy inside, at least till I remember Charles is here too."

"I think, I think you are going to have to get right with this Devon. I think Charles is going to be a big part of my life, much like you are. Maybe I could stop it from happening but I don't think I should. My gut says I need him the same as I need you."

He growls at me, "I don't have to like it yet. But I will find a way to tolerate it for now. What do you have planned for today? Or do you have plans for today?"

"I need to check in with Natasha and Memré, see how things are going with everything I left in motion when I had to leave so abruptly. I also want to get together a plan of action for training with my Dad. Decide if I go alone—"

"No." I narrow my eyes at him and he revises his interruption, "I mean, I would very much like to go with you."

With a wry twist to my lips I go on, "So I need to decide whether it will be just you going or if Charles will decide to come along as well. That is as far as I have gotten. I still need coffee."

A knock sounds on our bedroom door and it opens, Billy sticks his head through, "Devon, it's training time. Let's go. Hi Fate, glad you're back, sorry to interrupt but I am hoping that Devon will have better focus today since you are home. Maybe he won't hit the walls so often."

I sit up, drawing the sheet with me to keep my chest covered, "He hits the walls? Are the walls ok?"

"The walls are fine, we had them magically reinforced

so that we wouldn't knock the basement out of this place. It happened not too long after you left, because we needed to keep people occupied and not running around wreaking havoc."

"Havoc? Yes, let's avoid that if at all possible. I think I have brought plenty of that to everyone's life."

Devon sits up, wrapping his arms around me from behind, "You are not responsible for everyone's actions nor is it your fault that they are after you. Anymore than it was your fault Charles kept murdering you." He kisses my neck and slides out of the bed as Billy closes the door. I watch as he pads naked over to the closet to put on some clothes. There is not an angle that man looks bad from and getting to watch as he dresses is the highlight of my morning so far. He walks over and gives me a lingering kiss before he heads off to practice. I get out of bed with a sigh, this is a much better way to wake up than wondering if Pru will be hovering over my bed trying to kill me.

Three

FATE

Downstairs I find Maria has left a note saying the coffee is fresh and she has gone to market. She even put a time in the corner, and happily that was only about 15 minutes ago. I get myself a big cup and fix it just the way I love it. I move over to the island to sit and take that first sip of glorious wake up. I think after my coffee I will check my office and see if Natasha is in there or if she slept in too. I hear someone walking slowly down the stairs, I look up as Charles enters the kitchen.

He smiles seeing me and I feel all tingly in my special places. "I'm looking for coffee, is there any left?"

I nod, pointing in the general direction of the coffee maker. I watch him as he prepares his coffee. Devon is more relaxed and takes his coffee black. Charles is less fluid I suppose? But more contained, like he is ready to pounce on something. He finishes preparing his coffee and walks over to the island, stopping next to me, "Is Devon going to be very upset if I sit next to you?"

"No, though I am a little surprised you are concerned with his feelings."

He sips his coffee and savors it for a moment with closed eyes, "Yes," he says as he sits on the stool next to me and slides it a little closer so our knees touch, "I confess, I am not overly concerned for his feelings on the matter. In fact, goading him rather makes my day. I ask out of care for your feelings on the matter. I don't want to make you uncomfortable. I would like to make you very, very comfortable."

I feel the blush creeping up my cheeks as I sip more of my coffee. "I can't say I am surprised. It would help if you goad him less while he adjusts to you being here."

He studies his coffee for a bit before looking back to me, "I think I could be a little nicer to him for a price."

"For a price? What? What are you trying to get now?"

"A kiss. Just one little kiss."

My pulse speeds up at the thought and his pupils enlarge as he smells the pheromones released into the air by my excitement. "I think, I think I can do that."

He smirks at me, "I think you would like to do that. A lot more than you are letting on. Will you keep me little Fate? Will you kiss me to keep Devon more comfortable and possibly open the way to our bond forming? What will you do?"

His words stoke the fires inside me, I can feel how

much he wants me to open that bond. To allow it to happen, to take him as a mate. I set my coffee on the island and I stand, walking over to stand behind his stool. He sets his coffee down and spins around to face me, I am standing in the vee of his open legs.

"Put your hands behind your back, don't put them on me. You asked for a kiss from me, no touching this time."

"So there will be a next time?"

"Shut up and put your hands behind your back." He does and I see him clasp his hands based on the movement of his shoulders. I step forward fitting myself between his legs and pressing my thighs against him as I lean forward. I move to the left and keep my lips just hovering over the skin of his neck, breathing gently on the skin I watch it pebble and I feel him grow hard. I lean back just a little, moving till my lips are a fraction of an inch from his. I can hear his heart pounding away and his breath coming faster, it turns me on more. I press my lips to his ever so gently. Sweet little kisses of lips meeting till he opens his lips and I deepen our kiss. Tongues warring with each other as I press my body against his. I kiss him till he begins to growl deep in his chest and that is my cue to withdraw. I step back and his hands shoot out to grab my arms, "No, don't stop."

I smile as I shrug, "You asked for a kiss. If you want more you will have to follow through on your end of the bargain. Now let go of my arms Charles."

His hands drop like I am on fire and I check, I am a

little. Damn it. I go back to my stool and sit, sipping my coffee again.

Charles turns around, "The kiss certainly did not disappoint. I am going to have problems walking for the rest of the day. But I will be less antagonistic to Devon. Are you the same in bed?"

"I might be."

"Don't think I didn't notice you letting the bond form there either. Does Devon know what you have decided?"

"Yes. We talked about it this morning, and a little last night. We also talked about my trip to the Underworld. He wants to go, I wasn't sure if you would want to go. You can, if you like but you are not obligated in any way."

"I would like to. In part because I would do just about anything to spend more time with you."

"In part? What is the rest of the reason?"

"It is two-fold. One, I want to help keep you safe. I am more ruthless than my counterpart Devon. I think I have a better chance of doing that than he does. The second piece is that it gives me more opportunities to convince you to kiss me."

"Oh." I smile at him, "You are going to have to wait. I need Devon to be more comfortable before I go further. I can assure you that we will," I lean towards him to whisper, "see just how long you can keep your hands to yourself while I do things to make your eyes roll back in your head." I lean back again just as he nears my lips, "However, right now there are things to attend to like my training with my Dad. Come to think of it, you should go downstairs and spar with Devon. That might be good for both of you."

Charles raises a brow at me, "If I go down right now he is going to know exactly what I have been thinking about up here." My eyes drop to his groin and the bulge there. I can't help it, I start to giggle. He gets a twist to his lips, "I have never had a woman look at my package and giggle. I am finding I really don't appreciate the feeling at all."

"It isn't your package that I am laughing about, I was laughing because I haven't concerned myself with what someone thought about my causing a hard-on in many years. I agree though. You should wait until that calms down before joining in. In the meantime, I am off to find Natasha. She and I have business to attend."

"Sure. Leave me here in pain."

I turn back to cup his cheek with a hand, "Poor baby." Then I give him a couple light taps and turn away, heading for my office.

Smack

I freeze at the slap on my ass, looking back over my shoulder I tell him, "That's not the right way to do it." I leave the kitchen as he says that he hasn't had any complaints before.

I open the door to my office and find Natasha having her coffee at the table in the private portion of the office. I take the seat across from her, "How is your morning?"

"Better than it has been recently. Today I have my

friend with me instead of missing. I suspect you know that and are just being polite. You would like to know how things moved while you were gone."

"You know me too well. I do care about your morning. But I really want to know how the foundation is going and if we found a house or anything else that happened while I was gone."

Natasha and I spent the next couple hours going over the progress made on the foundation, which amounted to paperwork filed. Then she started telling me about the house and its current inhabitant. I told her buy the house, if the ghost has already approved of this wild menagerie, then it works for me. We set a tentative schedule for the week, based around my going to train four nights a week.

Leaving the office to head downstairs for lunch we run into the boys coming up the stairs shirtless and sweaty. Billy crosses behind Devon and Charles to get to Natasha. I walk over to stand in front of Devon and Charles who both flex a little. Having two men trying to outdo each other could turn out really nicely for me. I tell them I will be ready to go to the Underworld as soon as they shower and get ready. I hug them both at the same time and kiss each on the cheek. I step between them and start down the stairs only to feel two hands smack my ass. I stop and turn to look at them, "Really?"

They both smile and shrug, the two of them are hot enough to set me on fire. I just laugh and tell them as I walk away, "Smacking my ass is not going to convince me to skip training. But you don't have to go if it bothers you..."

I hear them both trudge up the stairs grumbling about seeing my father again so soon after he called them names and I laugh all the way to the kitchen.

Four

FATE

TWO HOURS later the boys are ready and so am I. At the last minute I ran upstairs and changed into form fitting workout clothing, just in case. I have no idea what the training Dad has planned will include. It is so weird calling Hades and Persephone my Dad and Mom. Walking back into the kitchen where Devon and Charles wait I am greeted with low whistles. I look up surprised as Charles says, "If that is what you look like when you are ready to train, we need to train more often."

"Much as I hate to say it, I agree with the blonde buffoon. Fate, you are smoking hot." Devin says before he grabs me by the waist and pulls me in for a lingering kiss. He releases me and before I can catch my breath Charles pulls me to him and kisses me deeply.

When he pulls his head back I step back slowly, a little shaky. "Did you plan that?"

They both answer, "No."

"Oh Sweet Lady am I in trouble. All right, we need to get going." I take their hands and close my eyes, focusing on being in the Underworld and seeing my father. I feel slightly disoriented for a minute and then I notice the sounds and smells have changed. Opening my eyes I look around and see that we seem to be in a huge cavern. Some spots are darker than others but where we stand is well lit.

I see a wide variety of people and creatures, then this giant three-headed dog comes running at me from across the way. The heads are all barking but they seem happy barks so I hold my ground even though I am worried he might not be as friendly as he looks.

I hear Devon whisper, "Holy shit, is that Cerberus?"

The dog stops just before plowing us all down, sits, puts its heads down and whimpers. I let go of the boys hands. Holding both hands out for the dog to sniff and he just butts them with his nose. I take a deep breath and reach up to pet his nose which is about what I can reach. He quickly tips his head so I can scratch the top of his head. Then he does this weird shake and gets smaller. This dog has three heads and changes size at will? I am in love. With his heads smaller I can scratch two of them. Which means I have to alternate because none of them want to be left out.

Charles asks, "Doesn't Cerberus translate to Spot?"

All three heads turn to him with a very serious look when he says Spot and he laughs.

I ask the dog, "Where is Dad at Cerberus?" He takes my hand in the mouth of the left side head and starts walking toward a well lit series of caverns. Once we step inside the appearance of a cavern is completely gone. This is a gorgeous mansion. All done in rich dark tones, each room a masterpiece in my eyes. We come to a closed set of doors and Cerberus pushes them open with a paw.

I hear wood splinter and my father start cursing Cerberus, "Dammit Cerberus, I told you to knock and I would open the damn door! Why can't you just knock?" Then he sees Cerberus dragging me in by the hand, "Fate! I am so happy to see you here!" He walks forward as Cerberus lets go of my hand, "I'll forgive you this time, I understand you were excited. It's ok." He pats all three of Cerberus' heads and the dog wags his tail happily. Then he pulls me into a hug, "I see you brought the idiots. Are they getting along any better yet?"

"Dad, don't call them that. It isn't nice."

He rolls his eyes, "Fine, I'll only call them the cretin boys."

"The cretin boys?"

"Yes. Cretin is another term for fool but is sounds nicer."

I roll my eyes at him and he laughs. "Fine Dad, call them cretins if you must. This place is beautiful. Is this where I was born?"

"Yes! Of course, but you wouldn't remember this

place... Let me show you around. This is still your house too. There is no place you are not allowed entrance, though some are more dangerous until you have fully activated." He loops his arm through mine, "Follow along Cretins, wouldn't want you lost. Cerberus might forget you are allowed here." I glance back to see the dog grinning at the two of them as they turn to follow us looking none too comfortable. I choke back the chuckles I know they would not appreciate right now.

Dad shows us the pool of rebirth, where the souls go when they are ready to live again. The blue of the water is so calming I almost want to go lay in it. Hades cautions against that, telling me that rebirth after becoming a goddess is not nearly so pleasant. Apparently you are fully aware the entire time.

We move on to the pool of cleansing. The waters are clear but the souls inside it are murky and angry, muddy black shot thru with red. Hades tells us that the souls in here have done things so heinous that even rebirth will not cleanse them and punishment is useless for them. Their souls have to be stripped bare and reset completely. It takes a long time and they spend a lot of time trying to leave the pool. Multiple times while he is speaking various souls attempt to leave the pool but make barely even a ripple as they are forced back down to the depths of the pool.

He leads us on, showing us the entrances to various sections of the Underworld.

Hades tells us, "For all that there are so many religions,

they all come here when they die. After so many come along complaining that they didn't get to their religion's place of rest I just go ahead and create one roughly based on what they collectively say it should be like and what ever literature I can find on the subject. It is fascinating sometimes. Others... not so much. There are a couple sets that are quite pushy about things and I ended up creating the punishment place they described so well for me. Now, let us show you to the family quarters. Try not to get lost Cretins."

I look back at the guys following along behind us and they smile tight smiles at me. I blow them a kiss and turn around to see as we enter a hallway. The hall is long and curves while rising gently. We come to an open space, painted walls and ceiling with images of the night sky. The stars seem to sparkle.

"This is the ball room. Your mother said once that it was beautiful and that we should put the entrance here so it wouldn't just be seen when we had a party. So I did."

"You have parties here? Balls with dresses and such?"

"We do. We would like to have one for you once your powers have fully activated and Demeter has been stopped."

"You would? We would dance here? In this gorgeous room? I would love that. But wait, who attends these?"

"Other gods, goddesses, and various immortal creatures in the know."

"That is a little intimidating. Will that be the first time I meet them? I don't know how I feel about that." I glance over at Devon and Charles, both give me encouraging thumbs up signs. "I'm sure it will be fine. Just nerves. Would I be able to bring friends?"

My father glances back at them and nods, looking back to me he says, "You are a Goddess, when your powers have fully activated you will be the equal of any of us. Not to mention, you are an amazing person, they will be lucky to meet you. You have so much of your mother in you, even if you have my emotional tell. And of course, bring whoever you like."

"Oh shit. Am I flaming again?" I look down at my hands and body as my father says that I am flaming again. I see the flames just barely covering me. I take a couple of slow, deep breathes to steady me and they fade into me.

"I think I am ready to continue now."

Dad shows me the rest of the family quarters which are palatial and have a gorgeous view of various forms of Summerland, depending on what window one gazes from. After the tour we head back to the area we entered the house from, but through the much shorter route of a hidden set of stairs. Dad takes us to a different room than the office type one he was in when we arrived, this one is huge and has a great number of obstacles, target walls, and what appear to be boulders on chains attached to various points in the ceiling. Those make me a little nervous but I can only hope he won't start me out with those.

Hades smiles and snaps his fingers, Cerberus comes running in. Looking at Devon and Charles he says, "Cretins, there is a path through the rocks over to the right, make it through or Cerberus gets an early dinner of you. By the way, he can make it through the course in twenty minutes, I suggest you aim for fifteen."

Their eyes go round and I wave my hand at them, giving them appropriate workout clothing as they take off at a run. My father turns to Cerberus, "Keep them on their toes, but no biting. She doesn't want them injured. But fetch them back here if you can. Make sure to drool on them a lot if you catch one."

I can't help but laugh as Cerberus takes off with a leap to chase the boys. I was frightened for them at first but knowing that Cerberus won't hurt them makes it hilarious. "Wait, what if they hurt Cerberus because they don't know? I don't want him injured either."

Hades laughs, "Don't worry. He is your mother's baby. No one can hurt him without some really heavy duty fire-power that they just don't have access to."

"Oh good. So, you aren't going to make me run through an obstacle course are you?"

"No. We need to focus on the further activation of your powers," he says as he leads me over to some target walls. "You are the prize that Demeter wants for her lover. Your mother," he looks away for a moment as his hands flame and curl into fists, "your mother was a fully activated goddess when they tried to push her soul from her body. That is why they were not able to, no matter what they did to her before she left her mother." His hands a bright blue balls of flame at this point and he throws them out in the direction of a wall, the flames shoot out from his hands in a long stream, hitting the wall and spreading to cover the entire thing. He closes his hands and makes a visible effort to calm his emotions. "You would think that after a few hundred years I wouldn't still feel so intensely about this but no. I can still see how badly they hurt her and remember how broken she was for so long because of what her own mother attempted to do. You have the flames that reveal your emotions the same as mine do. It is likely you can throw flames as well. Give it a try. Remember, they are connected to your emotions, the stronger emotions will produce stronger results."

I look at my hands and try to call up an emotion but I freeze. I can't think of anything. Hades sees this, and he starts talking, "When Demeter and her lover realized that your mother was out of their grasp forever they tortured and eventually murdered some of her maidens in an attempt to make her come running. I can only imagine what kind of things they would do to your family on earth in order to bring you to them. How they would terrorize them and hurt them over and over in your name. Telling them it would all stop if you would just give the word..."

By the time he finishes speaking I have managed to channel the flames to my hands. Raising them, I can barely see the wall for the tears in my eyes, I open and close my hands at the walls and I hear more than see balls of flame hitting the walls in succession. My flames calm and die down after many shots. The idea of someone hurting my family, I couldn't bear it.

"They are very likely to attempt to take out your family

to get to you. As soon as your mother gets back, she will teach you the protections she put on Cerberus," he smiles, "Oh look, here he comes now."

I turn to see Cerberus trotting over proudly hanging a very soggy Charles from one mouth with Devon trailing behind him. He drops Charles at my fathers' feet. Charles slowly gets up, drool dripping off of him in stinky puddles. Devon comes to kiss my cheek, and I try not to smile. I hold my hand out and materialize a towel, "Here you go Charles."

He accepts it with a nod of thanks, walking off a little ways to dry himself while he gives Cerberus the stink eye. Cerberus' right head seems to be grinning at him while the left nudges me for scratches. I oblige him, and he nearly knocks me over pushing his head at me. My father watches with great amusement as Charles dries himself.

When he rejoins us after dropping the towel on the floor my father assesses the two of them, "What did you do wrong? Why did he catch you?"

Devon shrugs, "I don't know. One minute I was running the course and next minute I heard Charles yelp. Then Cerberus trotted by with him."

Charles glares at Devon, "We didn't work together. Each of us took the course with no thought for the other making it easy to divide and conquer."

Hades nods, "Well, there may be hope for you yet. Again cretins, learn from your mistakes and do better. Her," he points at me, "life is on the line. If you cannot defend her then what is the point of you? Go."

The two of them take off running to the course again. My father strokes the middle and right heads of Cerberus, "You are the best puppy ever. Go chase them again, same rules. Extra drool."

I laugh as the puppy hops off toward the course, in the style of a certain cartoon skunk. When he gets to the course he stopping bouncing and begins stalking. He must be terrifying to be chased by.

My dad looks back to me, "Now, let's see what other tricks have appeared up your sleeve."

Hours later we leave, with a promise to come back in a days time. The boys have run the course multiple times and both have been brought dripping to my father by a very proud Cerberus. To their credit, it did take longer each time for him to catch one of them.

For my part, we spent our time working on offensive talents, measuring just what I was currently capable of doing. Dad said he would have a better game plan when I came back. He also said it was nearly time for my mother to come back from her 'visit' with her mom. I can't wait.

AJAH

I lay in wait for Ryna, I can smell her coming this way. I know she is searching for me, but it isn't training if I just let her catch me. And since that is what we said we came down here to do, well, we should train some. She has been hunting humans too long, she doesn't use her nose as effectively as she could. She is nearly to my hiding spot, I know she is tracking my heartbeat.

I wait till she is in just the right spot and pounce on her as she looks up and spots me. We roll with the landing and she stops us with her on top of me, "That was a dirty trick Ajah! How did you know I was coming that way?"

"I keep telling you, I can smell you. Fighting shifters or with shifters is different. We use every sense available. You have gotten lazy hunting humans and you don't use your sense of smell."

She nods, "In my defense, some of them are less than hygienic, the smell is not ok."

"I know, there are some of those in every species. And some that use that as a defense. So you need to use your nose. Do I get a reward for pouncing you so quickly?"

Ryna grins at me, "Will a kiss suffice? Or will you beg for more?" She asks as she leans down to touch her lips to mine. I deepen the kiss and wrap my arms around her.

She tastes like honey and I have a sweet tooth. We come up for air and I tell her, "Definitely beg for more."

Running my fingertips lightly down her spine to stop cupping her sculpted bottom I squeeze them lightly as I lean up to kiss her again. With her distracted by kissing me I slide my hands underneath her loose fitted dress and stroke them up her body to her braless breasts. I love that she rarely ever feels the need to wear a bra and I get to reap the benefits as I stroke her nipples in slow, light circles as they harden and she moans into my mouth. Lightly pinching her erect nipples has her pelvis grinding into me. I slip one hand down her belly and into her panties, she lifts ever so slightly to allow me access to her clit. I slide my finger between her lips and past her clit, just lightly grazing it as I seek the wetness from her core that will make this better for her. She breaks the kiss to breathe, both of us breathing heavy as I slip two fingers into her and she clamps down on my fingers. Following her lead I pull them back far enough to circle her clit and get it slick before I slide the two fingers back into her make sure to graze her clit with the base of my palm as I pinch a nipple and nibble her neck. I move my fingers in and out, curling them slightly to hit her g-spot and rubbing her clit steadily with the palm of my hand; within minutes she is humming on my hand. Her core squeezing my fingers in a staccato rhythm as she rides my hand. She falls limp on top of me, I start to move my hand and she convulses, "Wait! Don't move yet! I can't take it." I smile into the golden hair covering my face as her breathing begins to slow. She eventually allows me to remove my hand from her dripping pussy.

I roll her onto her back, "I want to taste you." I tell her as I sit up and grasp the sides of her panties, slipping them down her legs. I slide my knees back and position myself on my belly, with my face just an inch away from the feast before me. I lick her from core to clit in one slow swipe and she moans, pressing her pussy onto my face. I smile as I gently circle her clit with my tongue. Her moans are getting louder as I start to suckle her clit ever so softly. Her hip begin to buck and I start flipping my tongue across her clit as I slide three fingers into her. Her bucking gets wild as she grabs my hair and pushes my face harder onto her clit while she rides my fingers. I suck hard on her clit and her whole body cums with a thump. She pulls my head away from her now too sensitive clit as she continues to ride my fingers.

Hearing the door to the training area open we both freeze and then separate to straighten our clothing. Not because anyone in this house won't be able to smell what we were doing, but because we don't enjoy being caught with our panties down.

I hear the footsteps of someone with a lot of mass, must be the bear shifter, Owen. I smell Charles' body-guards, Rico and Benny. It isn't a bad scent but they love spicy foods and eating so they generally smell of the fiery spices. We get ourselves sorted well before they come into view, much to Rico and Benny's dismay.

"I told you the bear was the wrong one to help us find them. He walks too heavy!" Rico says as he bumps shoulders with Owen who laughs.

Benny raises his eyebrows at him with a skeptical look on his face.

I look Rico up and down saying, "You should worry about all the chilies you eat first, I can smell you and Benny for a mile. Owen was not the first clue that you all were here." Benny and Owen laugh loudly as Rico shrugs and smiles. So what if they weren't the first clue that someone was in here, they don't need to know the door tipped us off.

Benny says, "We came down to train but," he inhales, "It doesn't seem like you were doing the same training we thought to do."

Ryna grins, "No worries boys, we are all done in here, happy training." She walks through them without a backward glance.

I just watch her go for moment as does everyone else, before I follow her out telling the guys, "Sorry boys, you have all the parts she isn't interested in."

They roar with laughter at the jibe and I hear them starting to train as we close the door behind us.

$$\mathcal{F}ive$$

PRU

"Wake up."

I am floating in a dark place. It is quiet and all my thoughts are settled and there is no anything but the warm darkness. I like it here so I ignore the voice telling me to wake up.

"Wake up wretched child! They will only be gone for so long! WAKE UP!"

My eyes pop open as I hear the voice yelling at me. The voice was outside of me, I look around be everything is fuzzy and my eyes feel a little dry. I blink a few times and still am not seeing anyone.

"Good. Now get up. Your jailers will only be gone for so long. You have to be up and ready to fight. They will never let you go. They have been doing things to you while you were sleeping. They want to keep their prisoner, their plaything. But you, you have a job to do. You have to repay Fate for all she has done to you. I will help you, but you must come to me first. Now get up out of that bed."

Fate! How could I forget Fate? Why was I so mad at her though? And it was so peaceful in the warm darkness, maybe just a little nap... As my eyes drift closed the voice shouts again, "No! It is the drugs! Take out the IV so you can think clearly."

What? I look down at my arms, there is an IV. I snatch it out of my arm, unworried about bleeding too much because everything else might be fuzzy but I know I am a vampire and I will heal quickly. I feel the warm darkness retreating now that the IV is gone, and there is some sadness about that.

"Good. Good. Now get up. Fate has your son, she has your life, the life you should have had. She has your friends and you must take it all back. Yes! It makes you angry to think of all that Fate has taken from you! Hold onto that anger, it will serve you well. Get out of that bed, and grab a weapon, your jailers are coming back. You must kill them or they will force you under the spell of their drugs again."

I sit up slowly, "But it was so nice in the warm darkness. I just want to go back. Let Fate have it all. I don't care anymore. Maybe I should find my own life."

I feel anger bombarding me, and an answering rage exploding inside me. Suddenly I remember. I hate them all! Those bastards did this to me. Get them, I'll get them.

Looking around I see that I am wearing a hospital

gown. Not a whole lot in this room. What can I use? The dresser! Yes! I can feel the glee coming from the voice as I pull a drawer out and take it apart. I keep the front panel and discard the rest. I can hear the footsteps of my jailer and I move over to be behind the door as it opens without being in danger of being hit by the door. I listen, waiting, waiting as they draw closer. The knob turns and the door swings in on silent hinges. I see my jailer's face change as they realize I am not in the bed. I swing the board in my hands, keeping an edge aligned with their throat. I forget my own strength and shove the wood straight through. Blood sprays everywhere as I watch the head roll across the floor of the bedroom and stop facing the far wall. While blood sprayed initially, after that very little bleeding happened. I drag the body fully into the room and shut the door.

"Good, good. Your clothing is in the closet. Change and get yourself out of here. Take one of Charles' cars and come meet me here."

I am left with my rage and an address I must go to as I rifle through the clothes in the closet. I settle for pants and a shirt, both in black. My purse is in there too, which is odd. I don't recall bringing it here. I feel another stab of rage, I want to hurt someone for this! Who locked me up in here? Why? Fate! It must be Fate! She was always jealous, jealous of me. I leave the room, feet still bare but I don't need shoes. I step carefully and search the upstairs rooms. The third one has what I seek, weapons.

I don't know who sleeps in here but they have an

arsenal and I need one. I take two knives, a handgun, and a few clips. The handgun I shove in my back waistband and the clips in a back pocket. The knives, well I am going to use them on my way out. Bullets won't kill vampires, but cutting off their heads will. Fate has me prisoner in Charles' house of vampires, so I am going to thin the herd as I go.

Leaving the room I step soft through the hall to the stairs, staying close to the wall. Peering around the wall at the top of the stairs I see it is deserted. Then I remember, I can blink to wherever I want. Holding the knives at the ready, I blink into Charles' room.

No one here, and it smells like no one has been here for a while. I blink into Fate's room, same thing. They left me here as prisoner while they went off on holiday?

"Yes, they are off having fun knowing that you are drugged into a coma and they need not fear your retribution. Show them differently! Show them how powerful you can be!"

Blinking into Charles' office I head straight for his desk. Opening drawers until I find the lockbox I am looking for. I know the keys are around here somewhere but I just snatch the box open. I grab the few stacks of bills and stuff them in various spots in my clothing.

My work done in his office, I blink into the kitchen, landing behind the cook. Using both knives I decapitate him before he realizes I am there. This one was a vampire too, one quick spray of blood and then not much else. This one must be older, he seems to be turning to dust. How sad for him. No one else is in the kitchen, but luckily I went over pretty much every inch of this house before they drugged me, I blink into a secluded spot in the garage.

I stand very still and listen, looking around with my eyes only, I don't see or smell anyone in here. Walking over to the key holder I check out the cars as I go. They are all high end cars, though not so flashy as one would expect of a drug dealer like my son.

I settle on a Lexus. It is a nice solid brand and blends in well. I catch sight of myself in a mirror and realize, I don't blend well. And I am hungry. I pick up the keys to the Lexus and shove them in my pocket. Blinking myself into the bathroom off the kitchen I clean off the visible blood. Wearing black was a good choice. I step out of the bathroom and stroll over to the refrigerator. Opening it I find bags of blood mixed in with the food. I grab a couple bags and shut the door. Biting into one I blink myself back to the garage, next to the Lexus. Pulling out the keys I hit the unlock button and flip through the keychain to see if there is a garage button some where. Not seeing it I open the car door and lean in to look, there it is.

Sliding into the seat I hit the button to start the car and then reach up to hit the button for the garage door.

"Good. Now get yourself here. I have plans for you and that sister of yours."

Six

FATE

WE WALK BACK out to where we landed when we arrived in the Underworld, Cerberus walks with me. I pet him as we walk letting Charles and Devon walk a little ahead. They aren't feeling very charitable towards Cerberus for some reason. Even with the huge pile of towels they used to dry off while we were here, they are both still rather sticky. With one last pat on his head I tell Cerberus bye and step forward to take the guys' hands. It is a struggle not to make a face at the feel of the drool coating them but I think I manage ok. Their faces say maybe I didn't. I close my eyes and think of home and my bedroom since I am certain that will be empty.

Opening them again I see the familiar walls of our bedroom and I am relieved. For all that I took us there I was still a little worried that I wouldn't be able to bring us back. Releasing their hands I realize it is really noisy today, why is it so noisy? The guys must have had the same thought because they head for the door to the hallway. We all head downstairs toward the noise. I begin to pick out words and phrases, oh no. No it can't be.

We make it to the commotion and everyone gets louder, each trying to tell us what has happened. Finally Ajah roars and cuts through all the sound. Everyone is silent and looking at her till Ryna draws their attention saying, "They might be better able to understand you if you speak one at a time."

Devon picks that moment to say, "Billy, you first. What the hell has everything in an uproar?"

Billy looks directly at me, "Her sister has escaped."

My fears have come to life. Pru is wandering the streets and likely still wants me to be very dead. I extend my awareness and reassure myself that she has not popped into the house before I slam a shield around it.

Everyone seems to be watching me, hope I wasn't making weird faces while I did that. "I shielded the house and she isn't in here currently. Devon, Charles, go shower off the drool. It is starting to smell." I struggle not to chuckle at the agreeing nods from the shifters. "The rest of you, I need food so follow me to the kitchen and we can talk quietly about it. Without shouting over each other." Devon and Charles didn't need to be told twice. They left for the showers I think almost before I finished getting the words out. I can't blame them. I would too, it really was starting to smell and I can't imagine it is any more pleasant being the one that smells. Natasha, Billy, Rico, Benny, Ajah, and Ryna follow me into the kitchen where Maria is just putting together a plate of tamales for me. Bless this woman, hiring her was the best thing we have ever done. Paying her well over what would keep her staying is the second. I thank her for the food and take it over to the island to sit. Everyone spreads out around the island and I point to Rico and Benny, "You two, I assume it was you that found out originally?" They nod, "Great. Tell me what you were told."

They look uncomfortable, glancing at each other. Benny finally shrugs and says, "She was drugged, just like she was supposed to be. Sleeping deeply and the mind witch has been saying that she seemed to be getting more peaceful, her thoughts less chaotic and not so focused on you. The orderly walked the witch out and when they came back, Pru killed them. She cut their head off with a board from a dresser."

My jaw drops, and Rico picks up where Benny left off, "She took the money from Boss's office and killed the cook too. Cook was old and man, he never hurt nobody. She just took off his head and walked through his ashes. No respect."

Rico turns away and Benny pats his back saying, "Cook was a father figure to Rico. He might be upset for a while. Pru left in one of the Boss's cars. The guys there, they cleaned everything up. They collected the ashes and put them aside, because cook was special to a lot of us. We are going to have a memorial for him. They said last they checked the tracking, your sister was heading north."

"North? I can't imagine why she went north. What could be there for her? She has never left the state. But then again, to my knowledge, she never killed anyone before today either. Thank you guys. You can go and get some rest, just stay in the house. You are safe here. We will figure out more in the morning and I will relay all this to Charles and Devon. Natasha and Billy, what news do you have for me?"

Natasha says, "Well, you bought a house today. Since there were no restrictions or mortgage companies to deal with and we had the paperwork drawn up already, it's done. Maggie brought keys by and we can move in when you are ready. Maggie says she went by and let the ghost know that we bought it and she seemed pleased. Now that your sister is running loose, do you want to get in there immediately or wait till things calm down?"

I shrug, "You know, ever since Charlie died things have been building to this fever pitch, and a little before he died if I am honest. So no, I don't want to wait. I want to get the place secured and move in. So that is your next task, get the security system people out there and, Ajah, Ryna, could the two of you oversee that project? I think you are least likely to be attacked by my sister but I can shield you before you go, so you will be safe either way." They nod agreement with my plan and I go on, "While you are there, see if there are repairs of any sort that need done. Make sure all the appliances work and, maybe ask the ghost. She might save you some work or just be thrilled that it is happening."

They nod and say their good nights, explaining that they want to be ready to go as soon as I get them shielded up in the morning. I call them back and go ahead and shield them now because it won't interfere with anything and it will save me getting up early.

The kitchen is a lot emptier and the house a lot quieter, Natasha and Billy have sat down across from me and we are discussing the house when Charles walks in and sits next to me. I bump shoulders with him and keep talking to Natasha while Maria brings him a plate of tamales. Devon comes in moments later and takes the seat on the other side, I bump shoulders with him too. He thanks Maria profusely when she brings over his plate. Digging in he casts glances over at Charles, eyeing him like he is going to take his favorite toy from him. Natasha and Billy are struggling with their amusement as they watch Devon. Charles eventually notices it too, only he also notices that Billy and Natasha are amused. So he does what any good asshole would do.

He scoots his stool closer to me. Loudly. Devon narrows his eyes and slides his stool closer. Charles grins and slips an arm around my waist. At which point Devon sets his fork down and slides his stool back just a bit before he grabs me around the waist, lifts me and deposits me into his lap. Then he picks up his fork and continues eating like nothing happened.

Natasha and Billy are beyond what they can stand.

They both start laughing loud and long, I join in because it is just too funny. Charles starts laughing and Devon blinks at all of us for a hot minute before he too starts laughing. He gives me a hug and sets me gently back on my stool. I share with the guys all that Rico and Benny told me. Charles is upset about Cook as well, I put an arm around him for comfort.

Devon focuses hard on his food but mostly ignores it so I reach over and give his leg a squeeze. Reward the good behavior, right? We talk about options and I decide I need to tell them about the new house. Natasha is looking at me and so is Billy, because there are so many things they can't say if I don't spill the beans.

"So Devon, you remember we were talking about needing a bigger space?"

"Yeah, now might be a really good time to find something, eh?"

"About that..." He turns to look at me more directly and I let my arm drop from around Charles to give him my focus, "I actually started the process of finding one, before this," I point behind me at Charles, "guy kidnapped me. I thought I would surprise you with a house and then buy it. But I had Natasha buy it for me today. Surprise. Natasha, Billy, and I were thinking that we could all go ahead and move over there so we could stop bending space and time so far out of shape here. Plus, it is a little more secluded. We can throw up some illusion spells to keep people from seeing strange happenings and Pru will have to work harder to find the place. Oh, and it is haunted. But she is totally ok with all of us, we just need to acknowledge her instead of pretending she doesn't exist or trying to get rid of her."

Devon looks over my shoulder at Charles, I glance back to see him shrugging. Devon says, "You were really going to surprise me with a whole house?"

"I think I kind of did. I mean, you are pretty surprised, right?"

"I... You have a point. I am surprised. On the whole, I think it is a great idea though."

The next morning after coffee and breakfast, I walk Charles to the Denali. "I'm sorry I can't be there with you for this."

"It is better that you stay here Fate. I would feel really bad about killing my own mother. She isn't likely to try to hurt me. But I will be prepared in case she does. The guys say my car is still heading north. It is very likely that I have nothing to worry about for now. You stay here, and be safe." He cups the side of my face with his hand and I close my eyes leaning into it a little.

"I do plan to stay here, mostly. I need to pop in to the Underworld and let Dad know what is going on. I won't have time to come down for a few days while we get moved. I am the only one that can operate the shield and no one goes in or out without my allowing it."

I reach up and cup his face with my hands, gently

bringing him down to eye level, "You stay safe too. Vampires can be killed. You know that." I press a quick kiss to his lips and he snakes his arms around me, lifting me up and deepening the kiss. When we come up for air I realize I have wrapped my legs around him and his cock is pressing into some very delighted spaces. I let my legs drop down slowly and managed to increase the pressure between us, "I think you are going to need to let me down."

"I will never let you down, but I will set you down. For now. We are going to finish this conversation in the very near future," he says as he leans forward a little and sets me back on solid ground.

"I agree. Very soon. Now go tend to business." I turn and walk back to the house listening to him get in the Denali. I open the shield when I hear the truck start to reverse. Stopping at the door I watch them drive away as I close the shield behind them. Opening the door I step into the house and find Devon standing in the entryway. He takes my hand, closing the door behind me he tugs me into the first sitting room. Shutting the door he locks it as I stand there watching him. Turning back to me he pulls me into his arms and kisses me hard. I love it and I give it right back to him. He breaks the kiss and drops to his knees to snatch my leggings down. He waits patiently as I lift one foot and then the other so he can remove them fully. Then he leans in and kisses my pussy just as thoroughly as he was kissing my mouth moments ago. My knees go weak and he grabs my ass to hold me in place.

He pulls away and stands up, much to my dismay. The dismay is short lived as he picks me up and puts me over his shoulder to stride across the room and gently set me back on my feet directly in front of the couch that he pushes me down on. He gets back on his knees in front of me and snatching my ass to the edge of the couch he buries his face between my legs, licking and sucking me a screaming orgasm in minutes. My flames cover my body again, an intense purple. He stands and opens his jeans shoving them down far enough to be out of the way. Before he can drop to his knees I reach out and grab the cock pointing at me, "Turnabout is only fair."

I lean forward and wrap my lips around his cock, running my tongue in slow circles around the head as I engulf it. I spend long minutes making his legs quiver while I play with the head before I finally take most of his cock in my mouth.

I move my tongue along the underside as I slowly pull back and that is when he puts his hands on my shoulders, "Stop, that isn't where I want to cum."

I suck lightly on the head, letting go with a pop and a grin. He growls at me as he drops back to his knees and lines himself up with me. He drives his cock into me hard and fast, his thighs stop only when they hit mine. He grabs my legs and places one in the crook of each elbow so he can slam in deeper. "Touch yourself. I want to watch you touch yourself while I fuck you."

I grin and run my hand down my body, watching his eyes follow the progress of my fingers, the flames add an acid trip element I never expected. I slide my hand between us, fingers on either side of his cock and he groans at the feel of fingers and pussy. Then I bring them back up to my hard little clit and start to rub slow circles. His pupils dilate as my pussy clenches on his cock while he watches my fingers start to make faster circles. I feel another orgasm building in me, I know it won't be long before I cum again.

Then he growls, "Cum for me now." My orgasm hits like lightening and the flames on my body explode in a purple white light, it runs through my whole body and leaves me a shaking, cumming, bundle of nerve endings riding the pounding waves of his cock. He slams into me and the spasms from his orgasm set me off again.

He lowers my legs down to the floor and leans forward, his hands on the back of the couch holding him over me. He starts to pull out and all my nerve endings go haywire, "WAIT." I cry out as I clamp my legs on his hips."I need a minute before you move more."

He chuckles, still keeping his eyes closed. A couple minute later things have calmed down and I let him pull out. He pulls his pants up carefully and then lays on his back on the floor with his eyes closed and knees bent.

I sit up and look down at him while I work on calming my flames down, "Are you going to do this every time you see me and Charles kiss?"

He cracks an eye open, "Would it bother you if I did?"

"Not a bit. But I might kiss him more. For the after

effects." He laughs and closes his eye again. "Are you going to be ok with this?"

Devon sighs. "I am ok with it. I just... I still feel a little jealous and possessive. I figure this is the best way to take care of that."

"Well, I don't disagree. What are you going to do when he and I eventually have sex?"

He doesn't even open his eyes as he says, "Fuck you better than he did."

***

"I have to go see dad. I'll make it quick but I need to let him know that I won't be there for the next few days while we get moved. I am going to leave the driveway open, in case Charles comes back, you all will need to watch the area because anyone will be able to walk in."

"Do you really need to go by yourself? I could go with you. Is it safe to go alone?"

"It will be fine. Cerberus will come running and I am only going to be there for a few minutes. You need to keep on with the packing. Maggie's husband's shifter moving company will be here soon too. I want to be back by then." I stop and turn to face Devon, placing a hand on either side of his face I kiss him. A soft, brief kiss. "It will be fine. You can let me out of your sight for this. I promise it will be fine."

With that said I end the argument by taking my hands off his face and leaving for the Underworld. As I said would happen, Cerberus is immediately at my side. Scratching his ears I ask him, "Do you have a spidey sense for when I arrive? Your timing is impressive." We walk in the house/cave and I ask Cerberus to show me where Dad is. He happily trots slightly ahead of me, one of his heads turned to keep me in sight and watch behind us. We find my father near the cleansing pool, watching it swirl and bubble as a particularly nasty soul tries to escape it.

He turns as we walk up, "Fate! So glad to see you! What brings you here? I thought you weren't due till tomorrow?"

"I wasn't. But things happened while we were down here yesterday and it is going to be a few days before I can come back. My sister," Hades raises a brow at me, "adopted sister that is, she somehow surfaced from the induced coma, murdered two vampires, and seems to be heading north. But we intend to get moved into a more secure location now. I need to help with that and keep my people protected."

"You do me proud. I have a gift for you. Come Cerberus, let's show her your spawn."

"Cerberus has babies? I thought Cerberus had a penis? There are more of him?"

"My boy here is not an anomaly. He has a few females of his species here that he breeds with and infrequently this results in offspring. His kind are not terribly prolific so the pups are few and far between. However, we have some juveniles. I tend to keep them here, until I decide someone worthy of their company or they are grown and ready to be on their own. The rest of their tribe still live in their dimension and we introduce the pups to there in case they want to live there. Most do, but a very few decide they want or need to stay here for whatever reason."

"I had no idea. So does Cerberus visit his offspring in the other dimension?"

"Regularly. He is a good father. Here we are." Stepping through a door into a section of Summerland we are greeted by two juvenile images of Cerberus. Five different females of his species saunter up slowly. I notice the females seem to have only one head until they decide to allow us to see all of them.

"Do they all have the ability to appear as though they only have one head?" I ask as I am mobbed by the two juveniles.

"No. That is a female only talent. I have never found out why. But the juveniles here are in fact, female. And they seem quite enamored of you."

"I noticed. Sit! The lot of you!" The two juveniles sit in front of me and lean their heads toward me for petting. I work at petting all six heads while my father goes on to tell me the names of the females, I greet each with a nod.

Then he tells me the the juveniles' names are Trust and Kindness. I love the names and I ask who are the mothers of such fantastic pups. The one called Genara steps forward claiming the pups as hers.

"You must be so proud, they are beautiful." She nods and grins at me, briefly showing all three of her heads. The pups inherited her dark brindle coloring as opposed to their father's jet black.

Hades says, "Tell them to pass for dogs."

"Dog." I say as I snap my fingers. They shrink and have one head each in the blink of man eye. I reach down and continue to scratch the visible heads.

"Tell them to lay down."

"Lay down." I say, snapping my fingers again. The dogs lay down at my feet. I decide to continue on, I don't know exactly what Dad hopes to find out but can't hurt to play along while I am here. "Fetch me a small rock please." Trust and Kindness take off running. Very shortly they are back, each one dropping a rock into my cupped hands. "Thank you. Will you roll over for me?"

I feel Dad watching as the two complete a roll over each. "Good girls! Can you stand for me? Put your paws on my arms." I hold my arms out in front of me and they stand, placing their front paws ever so gently on my forearms. "Thank you. You can sit down now."

The pups sit and I look over to Hades. He nods at Genara who nods back. "When you get moved, your first visit here after that, these two will be yours. You will be their caretakers and they yours. Come, let's go back in the house. You will see them soon. Their mother wants to give them some extra tips and pointers while you get moved."

"Oh, bye darling girls. I will see you soon. I plan to come back for training as soon as possible and you can come home with me then."

As we walk back through the house I ask, "Not that I

am unhappy about the gift of Trust and Kindness, but why did you give them to me today?"

"It isn't very likely that your adopted sister woke up on her own. And that being the case, I have to wonder if Demeter hasn't been aware of your location for a long time. That would explain the way you grew up, how your parents suddenly turned on you and wanted to bind your powers. So I want you to have extra protection. Also, that soul in the pool when you first arrived? That was one of your mother's handmaidens. I don't know what they did to her but she is nothing like the innocent that was made to follow after your mother for many years. I think the likelihood of her recent death and your sister waking from a drug induced coma being coincidence is astronomically low."

"Oh. I guess that puts a new spin on things. Ok. Well, I need to go home. I left the gate open since I wouldn't be there and the movers were coming. I want to get back and get it closed. And I think I maybe need to convince Memré to move in with us too. I don't think Pru would hesitate to murder her just to get back at me."

Hades hugs me tight, "You be careful, be safe, and keep practicing your magic. Use it for everything. The more you use it the faster it will respond to you and the sooner you will be fully activated. Once you are fully activated it will be much more difficult for her to kill you." He releases me and put his hands on my shoulders, "I don't know if your mother can take you dying again. I feel like she is on an edge, ready to do some things specifically forbidden. Things that will cause a war between the gods. No one needs a war between the gods, it would decimate humanity and the consequences for the gods would not be much better."

"I didn't know it could get that serious. What is mom thinking of doing?"

"Killing her mother."

"Well... I kind of understand why she would want to and I mean, based on the myths I have heard, that is kind of a done thing in the world of gods."

"It was. And Zeus lived in fear of that very thing for many years. So eventually we all got together and brokered a deal that any child killing their parent would be subject to the death penalty. If the parent was that horrible then they had to go through the system we created for handling these things. Only, our system is flawed and run by those who were in power then. Those that seek power and curry favor with Zeus. Secondly, it wouldn't just be a war of the Greek pantheon. And Zeus is not the most powerful of the gods, in any pantheon, though he styles himself so."

"Oh, so like the saying, 'A lion doesn't have to tell you it's a lion."

"Yes. Now go and be cautious, stay alive."

"Yes Dad." I say as a snotty teen joke and he crushes me in another hug.

He releases me and wiping the corners of his eyes he says, "I really missed getting to hear things like that. I love you, be vigilant. We can't lose you again."

I close my eyes and think of home as tears slip down my cheeks.

Standing in my bedroom I think for a moment to recall where I left my phone. Not recalling the location I just hold my hand out and call the phone to me. Dad told me to use my magic as much as possible. My phone appears in my hand and I tap the screen a few times, unlocking it and pulling up Memré's number.

"Fate! I am so happy to hear from you. Are you having the honeymoon you never had?"

"Well, not exactly. Things have gotten complicated, but I am having a lot of really great sex. That isn't what I called about though."

"Oh. Well that sounds serious."

"It always is. Pru woke up from her induced coma, killed two people and took off in one of Charles's cars. We have good reason to--"

"Believe that she will be back trying to kill you any minute now?"

"Well, yes. Exactly. But not just me. I have a plan to protect myself and everyone else. Which is easier because of proximity."

"Let me stop you right there. I am not moving into that little house. It is stuffed to the rafters. Nothing good is going to come from distorting so much space like that. I don't want to be there when it turns into a black hole or something else equally disastrous."

"Then you will be glad to know I bought a giant place that has all the rooms we need without distorting things.

You would have your own space. The best internet I can get piped in there, safety, and access to Maria's cooking."

"Maria is still there? She would make food for me too? My own space? Like a suite of rooms?"

"Yes. I bought a giant old mansion. It's even haunted. The ghost is apparently really nice, she just wants to be noticed. What do you say? You could make money renting your place out, I know a great property management company."

"Fine. I am not bringing any furniture though, ordering it all. Send your moving company friends by to pick up my boxes too. I'll insta cart boxes to the house and get packed today. You do mean now, don't you?"

"I do. I don't know how long we have before Pru goes on the attack. I want everyone in the new place so I can lock it down magically. The spell I am thinking is going to be pretty complicated so I am calling Griselda. I need help getting it sorted so it does what I intend."

"All right. I need to get off here. I have pants to put on now, and boxes to order. I'll see you later. Don't forget to send them for my boxes."

"I'll send them. Thank you. I want you to be safe."

"I know. And I know your sister is a grade A whack-a-doo right now. See you later."

Seven

MEMRÉ

IN THE TWO days since Fate called me to move into this house, everything has been a whirlwind. I packed my things and the moving wolves, it still makes me chuckle how much they did not appreciate being called that, arrived at my house about the time that I finished. She had a bed here waiting for me when I arrived but left everything else to my discretion. Things like this are why she is my friend. She knows I value my independence. Fate knew I would balk at moving in with the crowd. She gave me a suite of rooms away from the main portion of the house and made sure it was a blank slate with the exception of the brand new bed. Even that she had placed on railings and nothing else, so that I would be able to choose the bed furniture. Of course, this means that my rooms echo for everything. First order of business, after some of Maria's waffles and coffee, is to get furniture ordered and delivered as soon as possible. I throw a robe on over my hearts and stars jammies, because comfort, and head out to the kitchen area. Happily no one talks to anyone that hasn't had coffee first thing in the morning. Of course morning is a relative term in this place. I haven't seen anyone keeping a schedule that included being awake during actual morning hours. To my knowledge Fate quit that when Charlie died.

I find Fate in the kitchen with Seamus, Ryna, and Ajah. Grabbing my coffee I am shooed out of the cooking area by one of Maria's helpers who tells me I'll get no breakfast if I stay underfoot.

I get to the table everyone else is sitting at and take my own seat, sipping my caffeine. Seamus' phone rings and he rattles off the address to the house saying he can't wait to see the person on the other end of the line. I raise an eyebrow at Fate, she waits till Seamus ends his call to tell me, "Looks like Malachi will be here today. This should be interesting. Seamus, is he still thinking of doling out punishments?"

Seamus suddenly becomes even more pale, "I believe so. He is reasonable. The problem is that you technically fall under his command as well, so you won't have a lot of pull with him."

Fate lets loose this wave of raw power that rocks everyone in the kitchen and sets everyone in the house running for the kitchen as she says, "I am under no one's jurisdiction. Not even an elder vampire. He would do well to realize that quickly."

By the time she is done speaking the kitchen has filled with people. Maria cuts the tension saying, "I don't care about jurisdictions. You throw power around like that and mess up my food, you're not getting any more of it."

Fate's mouth drops open and she hurries to apologize to Maria saying, "I am so sorry, I didn't intend for that to happen. Forgive me?"

Maria nods and goes back to cooking, muttering under her breath. Those with supernatural hearing laugh so I can guess she must be saying some hilarious things.

I do have questions of my own so I ask, "Who is this guy anyway?"

Seamus answers, "Malachi is mine and Ryna's father of sorts. He found us when we were orphaned children a very long time ago. He raised us as his own and kept being a vampire secret from us until we were near grown. He only told us then out of necessity. Ryna and I spent a long time discussing it and we eventually decided that he was going to make us vampires too. He did not appreciate the idea. It took us five years and another vampire on standby to do the job if he refused before we were able to convince him. It was much later that we realized how much danger we had put that other vampire in by pitting him against an elder. The other vampire was not aware of who our father was, and truth told, we obviously weren't fully aware either. An elder vampire is one of the original few vampires. No one knows which of them is the original but they laid down the law long before we came along.

"Once upon a time younger vampires were killing humans left and right, it was bad. The elders got together, created a set of rules and then enforced them for about twenty years before they could go back to their own lives. Everyone had the fear of the elders in them by then and the system was in place. Those who didn't follow the rules set down were usually dealt with in a very harsh manner by the vampires around them to avoid the notice of the elders. So he is one of the elders and as such he is a vampire ruler, so to speak." Seamus glances at Fate and amends his words, "At least of most vampires."

"If I understand you correctly he is just one of a few really old guys that took over when vampires didn't behave and deemed themselves the overlords?"

Ryna pales this time, "Please don't say it to him like that. He very much will not appreciate it. He doesn't like to think of himself that way. He really is quite powerful and I don't want to see him angry at any of you."

I look across the table at Fate, she nods at what she knows I am thinking. Knowing she agrees that this sod won't get to push anyone around for any reason. If nothing else I can drop him in a hole and close it over him. However, it would seem my Fate has grown in strength recently if that blast was anything to judge by, I may not need to do anything. Except laugh when she puts him in his place.

One of the shifters, I still haven't learned all their

names, brings a guy into the kitchen. This guy is magnetic. Rugged good looks and looks intelligent. I feel things waking up that I have kept shut off for a long time and that kept my life better for it. So he is someone to be avoided. Then Seamus and Ryna greet him and I realize that he is Malachi. Oh no. He is going to be here. Oh no.

"Fate, Memré, and Ajah, we would like to introduce you to Malachi. Malachi, Fate is Devon and Charles mate, Memré is Fate's long time friend, and Ajah is a bodyguard, friend, and Ryna's girlfriend." Seamus grins at Ryna as he rats her out with the last bit. Ryna smiles so sweetly at him that I am a little afraid for the boy.

Malachi nods to each of us saying, "It is very nice to meet you all. Did I hear that correctly? Did you say Fate is now the mate of Devon and Charles? Both of the men I am here to investigate?"

Seamus nods, "Um, yes. Let's have a seat. Things have changed a bit since we sent the message to you. There is a lot more to the story than we, any of us, originally knew."

"We can sit but I don't know how much the story will change anything. I am going to need everyone that isn't a vampire to clear out. This is vampire business and we don't need witches," he looks me in the eye and I narrow mine at him, he moves on to Ajah who sits up and leans forward, "or shifters in vampire business."

Fate's hand curls into a fist as blue flames spring up over her entire body. No one has narrowed eyes anymore but Malachi hasn't realized the danger he is in as he continues to try to stare Ajah and myself down.

Fate stands and draws his attention as she leans forward a little, placing her hands flat on the table. "Malachi, I am going to pretend that you have been out in the wilds for too long and forgotten your manners. As your son said, things have changed. Not only with what we knew about Devon and Charles situations, but also with the world in general. First, you need to know, you are not in charge here, you have no say in who stays or goes."

The poor fool opens his mouth and says, "Who do you think you are young lady?" Or at least I think that is how it was going to finish, Fate cut off his ability to speak or move. The flames coursing over her are much bigger, and I am a little concerned for the house, though the table seems fine.

Malachi stops struggling and Fate continues when he looks to her, "I don't appreciate being interrupted, especially by a guest in my home. I am the fucking goddess of the house. For that matter, I am the goddess of this area. I offer you hospitality, but I will not allow poor behavior. As for your judging of Devon and Charles, they are mine. Both have made mistakes as far as regards the rules your and yours set up. But if you are not capable of listening to the entire story and acting accordingly in a compassionate manner, well, I suggest you leave while you are able. And lastly, we do not separate species in this house. We are a fucking team, period. You don't have to agree with it but you will respect it in this house. Are we clear?"

Amazingly enough his face changed as he listened to her and at the end of Fate's tirade he nodded his agreement.

She waves a hand at him, clearing whatever she used to get him to listen quietly.

"My apologies Fate. It has been a long time since someone put me so thoroughly in my place." He looks around the table, "Perhaps times have changed and I should put away old prejudices. I am willing to listen to the entire story of Devon and Charles, and I will be compassionate with a caveat, only that they haven't caused any large scale damage. Most things can be overlooked but the whole reason for the rules was to prevent large scale loss of life."

Fate sits down, the flames much smaller but still there, "I think we have no worries there. To my knowledge they were both relatively circumspect in their feeding as well as their killing. I believe Charles killed more than Devon, but he has been a drug lord for a long time, so I think no more than would be normal for that line of work. Which is likely less than you would be concerned with I believe."

"Well, yes. That is less than I am concerned with though I actually meant more along the lines of mass murder type occurrences."

"To my knowledge, there hasn't been any of that. For now though, you have traveled a long way and Charles has not come home yet. Why don't Seamus and Ryna show you to your room, as I am sure you would like the opportunity to spend time with your children first, yes?"

I watch as Seamus and Ryna lead him away, I bet I could bounce a quarter off that butt. He is hot as can be but his whole personality ruins it. He seems to think he is entitled to rule by virtue of being old. Fate on the other hand, recently found out she is a literal goddess but she was willing to beg me to live with her for my safety. I would like to think it was due to the times that he started out in except he has no issues with the electronics or cabs or planes, none of which existed back when he was born. That is a shame. I might have been willing to break my dry spell for someone as hot as he is, against my better judgement as it would have been. But that kind of entitlement? I just don't have the energy to train that out of someone. Not even for a butt I could bounce a quarter off of.

FATE

Charles arrives home a few hours after Malachi's exciting arrival. He has been gone for a few days, but stayed in contact. When he arrived he sent me a text asking where I was hiding, I replied that I am in my office. Knowing full well he has no idea where that is. When he sent back that he was coming to find me and I better stay put, I did. I stayed right here in my office and laughed while I worked at setting it up how I please.

I am in the middle of moving a couch with my magic when Charles enters my office, spins me around and lifts me up for a kiss that sets me on fire, literally too as my flames flared all over and I felt it happen this time. He doesn't seem in pain so I ignore my flames as I wrap my arms around him and kiss him for all I am worth. When he breaks the kiss and lets me slide back down to set my feet on the ground I can feel his cock straining to be free of his pants.

We are both breathing heavy and his eyes are nearly black. He grabs me by the waist and puts me up against the wall, pressing his lips to mine as my legs wrap around him of their own volition. He grinds his cock against the juncture of my thighs as his kiss becomes almost punishingly hard. I give as good as I am getting, one hand gripping his hair and the other digging in the muscles of his back. My legs have him trapped, pressed tight against me where his every movement sends electric shocks through my body.

I hear a noise and break the kiss, breathing heavy I say, "We can't do this right now."

Charles smiles and he looks more like the tales of vampires out to steal the innocence and the blood of the fair maiden when he says, "Oh, but we could. We could shut that door and I could make you scream my name." He thrusts just a little and I moan.

I don't hear anyone nearby so I use magic to quietly swing the door closed and then seal the room to keep anyone from coming in as well as prevent any sound from leaving the room.

I let the couch sink gently to the floor as Charles starts kissing me again. He lets go of my waist and moves his hands to unbutton my shirt, making quick work of it and my bra. He cups my breasts and then pinches the nipples, I break the kiss to gasp enough air to moan, he says, "Oh, so that's what you like? A little pain with your pleasure? Let's see what this does for you."

He holds me against the wall as he steps back, I release him and let my legs swing down toward the floor. He lowers me till my feet are flat on the floor and leans in to take a nipple in his mouth, sucking hard on it for a moment before releasing it to lave it with his tongue, alternating licks with nibbles. His hands are busy removing my pants and thong. The cool air on my pussy feels nice since all of me is on fire.

"The flames don't bother you do they?"

He releases my nipple from his mouth, and I look down to realize he has divested himself of all his clothes too, and those suits of his have been hiding a sizable package. He notices where my gaze has gone and smiles that cocky smile of his, "No, the flames just make me realize I have never tasted flaming pussy."

He drops to his knees and plants his lips at the front of my pussy, slipping his tongue between them to rub my clit. My legs part for his face and he slips his mouth down to suck on my clit hard till there is just an edge of pain and my knees nearly give out. He slaps a hand on my belly holding me up against the wall as his mouth does wonderfully obscene things to my pussy. Then, just as I am swimming on the edge of a mind blowing orgasm he slips his thumb into my pussy and presses my back passage with a finger while sucking hard on my clit and my orgasm explodes in sensation and light. My pelvis rocking on his hand while my thighs shake and the only thing keeping me upright is his two hands, one of which has a thumb and a finger buried in my spasming body.

He lets go of my clit and my body begins to calm down until he moves the digits inside me and sets off another wave. He slowly withdraws them and stands, slipping an arm behind me he slides the hand on my belly down and then behind my knees, swinging me up into his arms he walks over to the couch and sets me very gently down.

On his knees again in front of me he takes my face in his hands and kisses me, lightly at first. As I come back to earth and respond the kiss becomes more.

I feel his cock stabbing at my ribs, I reach out and take it in my hands, he breaks the kiss and sucks air like a man starved for it. I grin as I stroke his cock and he rests his head on mine, moaning for me to please put it in.

I lean back a little and line his cock up to my entrance, pulling him ever so slightly forward till he begins to enter my soaked pussy. That is all the encouragement he needs and he slams into me. I grab the edge of the couch and hold on tight as he slams into me over and over, my head falling back as he leans down to kiss his way down the side of my neck. He reaches the spot where neck and shoulder meet, biting and drinking lightly from me but increasing my pleasure till I break again, the light show is near blinding. My orgasm and the taste of my blood in his mouth send him over his own edge as he slams into me again, I feel the throb of his cock inside me as he spills his seed.

He lets go of my neck, the holes close even before he

can lick them to add to the healing. I release the edge of the couch and fall back to rest on the cushioned back, he leans forward to rest his head on my shoulder saying, "Finally. I knew I would get in your pants one day." With a sly little grin.

"Ego much? Ugh. Get off me sir. I still have work to do and someone will be looking for me soon enough."

He grins and pulls out of me slowly enough that it causes my eyes to roll back in my head. He takes my hands as my eyes open and helps me stand again. My legs are a little wobbly but they work. I decide to try magic for putting my clothes back on, I snap my fingers while focusing on them being in the correct places and it works.

"Yes! Want some help getting dressed?"

Charles raises a beautiful blonde brow at me and says, "Why not?" with a shrug.

I concentrate on his clothing, making sure to get the image just right because I am not familiar with his clothing, and snap my fingers again.

His clothes are on him and appear to be in the right places, "Is it right? Nothing on backwards or sideways?"

Looking down at himself he say, "Yes, it all appears to be in the right order. Good job. Might want to open a window and send the smell of sex out, before you open the door there."

"Oh, yes. Devon is still a little twitchy about you, I don't want him more uncomfortable."

Using magic I open the window and have the air circulate through, clearing out the aromatic evidence. I pull

down the sound barrier and have the door swing open as I
go back to moving the couch where I wanted it.

"So, did you get everything taken care of at your
house?"

He sits on the couch in the spot I recently vacated and
says, "Yes. I arranged for a couple of the guys to handle
the business, they will keep me informed. All the mess and
evidence of Pru's escape is gone. The doctor says she had
to have had help of some kind. She could not have come
up on her own, they had her meds at the optimal levels.
The mind witch said she was doing better. Calmer and
things were falling into place. Then she woke up and killed
two people on her way out. But who could help her
without being there?"

"I don't know. I can't imagine who would? Admittedly," I say as I move my desk again because it isn't quite
right, "I don't think I knew as much about her as I thought.
Maybe she has a bunch of people willing to help her
escape. I wish I knew why things are so wrong between us.
Why our parents— Never mind. That stuff doesn't matter.
We'll find her and figure out who did help her and we will
get her back into treatment. Hopefully this won't set her
back much. Did the doctor say anything about that?"

"No, he—"

Devon knocks on the door as he walks through, and he
smiles at me, "How are you beautiful?" As he walks over
and takes me in his arms, kissing me silly. When he breaks
for air he smirks at Charles who smirks right back.

I roll my eyes at the two of them, "Any rate, what

brings you up Devon? Did you miss me? Or is Malachi wandering about trying to assert dominance again?"

"What? Is Malachi here? I haven't seen him. No, it is nearing dinner time, I hoped to convince you to come down and have a drink with me, you too Charles."

Charles raises his brows, "I would love to have a drink with the both of you. If you weren't such a good guy I would worry you were trying to poison me."

Devon smiles, "You're safe. For now. You, however, are not safe. I have plans for you later that won't include him, well, beyond him getting to hear you make those delicious noises..."

I blush because I know Charles is thinking about the noises I just made for him. Thank goddess Devon can smell very little. "I would love to have a drink with you and Charles. It would be a wonderful thing if the two of you could get along."

Devon takes my arm and we walk out with Charles following as Devon says, "I am well aware of what happened in there before my arrival. We already spoke about what will happen later."

His grin has me blushing again. Sweet Lady, how am I going to keep up? Then again, it isn't me who has to keep it up, ha. We get to the staircase and Charles steps up beside me, taking my other arm. Walking down the staircase with my two vampires, it just feels so right having the two of them at my side. We head directly for the salon with the liquor cabinet. Our ghost lady has been incredibly quiet so far, no one has seen her. But certain things indicate she is around. Like the liquor cabinet. It looks like a plain bar from both sides, not even storage. Until you touch a particular spot and the doors open. When we were first exploring the house, I set my keys and phone on the bar. The keys slid across the bar to the hidden button and the doors opened. I said thank you and showed everyone where to find the button. Lots of little things like that have happened here and we all just take it in stride. I hope she will eventually show herself, I am curious to know her.

Devon goes behind the bar and pulls out a bottle Belvanie and a bucket of ice. I sit down in one of the chairs while he makes drinks and Charles takes the one across from me. Devon delivers our drinks and takes the chair closest to me. I ask Charles, "So what did the doctor say about Pru?"

He shrugs and sips his whiskey, "Just that she could not have come out of that without help. He suggested that perhaps her desire to hurt you was not all her own if someone was willing and capable of waking her up out of that coma. I told him we would be extra cautious about you. So who is Malachi?"

Devon answers, "He is one of the vampire elders. Did you know there are rules to being a vampire?"

"What do you mean rules?"

I pipe in, "Oh yes. In fact, I found a copy of the rules in The Chronicle, you broke quite a few when you made Devon a vampire."

Charles raises a brow, "Was I supposed to get permission? Because if so, I broke that same rule with you."

Devon answers him saying, "No. Permission isn't mentioned, but we are responsible for those we create. We are supposed to train them and keep them out of trouble for the first twenty years. Keep them from going on a killing spree or revealing our existence."

"Really? I was about a minute old when I turned you. My father had turned me just recently and all I could think was that you had to be a vampire too or you would never live long enough for me to exact my revenge. Everyone else I turned much later and they were all kept near so I could monitor them, for much the same reasons laid out in the rules. And it is difficult to maintain a financially lucrative drug operation if your employees kill everyone. One guy did go nuts, he was put down quickly. But we were in the middle of a cocaine operation. I attributed it to that."

I shake my head, "Wow. Yes, really about the twenty years. I think Malachi will be willing to see reason about this. You couldn't have known." We all get the message from Maria that dinner is ready. I stand, downing the rest of my whiskey. The men do the same and we all set our glasses on the bar as we head for the dining room.

Eight

FATE

DINNER TOGETHER WAS INTERESTING. Malachi wanted to talk information on Devon and Charles, and for a brief moment thought he would sit at the head of the table. He really is a pushy sort that want to dominate a space. Happily, it doesn't seem to have anything to do with me being a woman, it is simply that he is unused to not being in charge.

I did agree that we could sit and have the discussion as soon as dinner was finished. Memré was unusually entertained by the clashes between Malachi and myself, he noticed it too, and I noticed him noticing her. I don't think she has noticed him watching her yet.

We all adjourn to the living area. Charles, myself, and Devon take up a large loveseat. Natasha and Billy share a chair, Ajah and Ryna on one end of the couch with Seamus next to them and Malachi next to the other arm, leaving Memré with the options of sitting next to Malachi or pacing. She chose pacing. Malachi's eyes followed her even as he said, "Let's start with you Fate, how did you become a vampire?"

"I was turned by Charles. Though Devon had already planned to turn me, but as you can see, neither one has any inclination to leave my side. Though admittedly, my training is coming from elsewhere."

"Elsewhere?"

"Yes. My parents are training me. Their training is rather… more than what is required for vampires."

"I'll be the judge of that. Who are your parents?"

"Hades and Persephone."

Memré had been wandering the room and happened to be at an angle to see Malachi's face when I told him my parentage, she burst out laughing, "You should see your face! All high and mighty one moment and then very serious oh." She grabs the mantle to help her remain upright, mostly, "I didn't know vampires could be that nonplussed! I need a drink, does anyone else want a drink? I can bring back drinks."

We all ask for drinks, and leave it to her to decide what to bring us. She is still laughing as she heads out of the room and Malachi is still watching her. Once he can't see her any longer he turns back to us, "I can see how your parents training would be beyond the requirements. I do have questions about why you are only now getting trained and why you were even turned, but they don't pertain to this. So we will set that aside for now. Devon, how did you become one of us?"

Devon cuts his eyes at Charles briefly, "I was turned by Charles as well, a little over two hundred years ago. He didn't stick around but I know now that he was not aware that he was required to train me. I didn't go on any killing sprees that would have revealed us to the humans, I actually faked my death and left the place where people knew me."

"I see. And you Charles? How were you turned?"

"I was at home one night, miserable as usual when my estranged father busted my door down. He stepped through mumbled something about never having done anything good for me and the one thing he could do was to give me the gift of time. The he bit me and drank me nearly dry before he slit his wrist and forced me to drink. Thanks for asking, lovely memory to recall. No, he did not stick around to teach me anything. Just left me there with a broken door and a lot of questions. Have I answered yours well enough?"

Malachi's face is very carefully blank, "Who is your father?"

"Judson, I know he still goes by Judson, beyond that, could be anything."

"I think I know who your father is. He was trained. I will need to check in with some contacts. Did you run rampant or go on a killing spree after that?"

"No. Surprisingly, I did not. The ones I killed, they

needed to die anyway. I was never overcome by hunger like one hears about."

Devon looks over at Charles, "I wasn't either. But even I have heard of those that were. Malachi, any idea why that would be?"

"That would be because of me, Cretins."

We turn at the new voice and then I jump up, "Dad! I am so happy to see you! What brings you here?"

"I came to bring you Trust and Kindness, they are outside checking the perimeter. But I happened to hear Cretin Devon asking his question and I knew I was the answer." He looks to Malachi, "I ensured that these two would be vampires. That you can lay at my door. Cretin Charles father not sticking around to make sure he trained his son, that's on him. I can only plant the seed. I have a day job so to speak."

"I understand. So these two were under your eye when they were new?"

"Yes. For some reason my wife deemed them accept-able for my daughter, and I must ensure they are worthy of her."

"I understand. Admittedly, I have been less concerned for Ryna since she came out. Not that women can't be trouble, but I feel like the expectations placed on them are higher from a young age and they are generally better people. Especially if my daughter is willing to be around them. She has better taste than Seamus."

"I can understand, though I will say, a soul is a soul. I

have seen evil come from all genders, some just hide it better."

"Point taken, I will keep that in mind. If you will excuse me, I will go let Memré know we have another here for a drink."

"Excellent. I do love a good drink." Hades turns back to me, "Shall I call them in to meet everyone?"

"Yes, though I haven't told anyone about them…" I turn back to face everyone, "So um, we got a couple of," I look back at Hades, "Are they dogs?"

"Close enough." He says as he smiles at Devon and Charles.

They say in unison, "Oh no."

I turn back to look at them, "Oh yes? Cerberus has puppies. Dad is gifting us two, for security. Their names are Trust and Kindness."

Charles rubs the bridge of his nose, "Oh for fucks sake. Fine. Fine. But, if we start that training program here, no surprise training. My suits take time to make and we are not ruining them regularly for your entertainment. However, we aren't the only ones that need to be better trained, are we Dev?"

Devon looks startled to be included in Charles conversation but looking at him he smiles wide and says, "I think you may be right this one time. Everyone should train that way, on a schedule. It will keep Trust and Kindness on their toes too."

Hades laughs as Memré and Malachi return with drinks. She looks annoyed and he does too but he is still watching her every move as she takes drinks off the tray he is holding and passes them to their intended recipient. Malachi follows Memré around the room, stopping in front of Hades and myself. She hands us drinks and when Malachi attempts to hand over the tray she looks down her nose at him, "You know where that goes. You are capable. Go put it back."

Malachi opens his mouth and closes it a few times until Hades starts laughing at him. Then he takes off out of the room, tray in hand. Memré turns to my father, sticks out her hand and says, "Hello! So nice to get to meet you this time. Has your lovely wife not gotten back home yet?"

He shakes her hand warmly, "Very nice to meet you as well. Sadly, she is not back just yet. But soon, soon she will be home and all will be right with my world again."

"Aw, I love that. You two are still in love after all this time."

"Even more than when we first met. But now, here are Trust and Kindness." As he says it they walk through the wall behind him.

Memré kneels down and sets her drink on the floor behind her, "Oh what darlings, would you come let me scratch behind your ears?" Trust and Kindness amble over and she quickly has two heads shoved under her hands.

Ajah, Ryna, and Seamus come around the couch to get in on the puppy scratches. As soon as Trust and Kindness realize there are a lot of hands waiting to scratch them, they each allow all their heads to be seen for optimal scratching. No one even bats an eye, they just spread out the scratches and coo at them about how beautiful they are.

Hades turns to me, "I seem to have accomplished what I set out to do. I will see you tomorrow for training again, yes?"

"Yes. I wouldn't miss it. I will bring Charles and Devon again, I wouldn't want Cerberus to get bored."

The twinkle in his eyes as he says, "Ah, you are a daughter after my own heart. I can't wait to see the things you get into when you have all your powers. My brothers, they went around breeding everything they could find, and it didn't work out so great for them. Most of their children are dead. Or imprisoned. I found your mother and have never strayed, we had one amazing daughter. I am so grateful we have you and I really can't wait for your mother to get to know you and start passing on her ideas. You two are going to have so much fun and those cretins aren't going to know what hit them. See you tomorrow." He pulls me in for a hug, releases me and disappears. His glass pops into place on the mantle with a little clink sound.

I look down and find Memré watching me, "I am so happy for you. You have always deserved so much better than the parents you had and I am just so glad that you have them now. Also, can we talk him into letting me have one of these? Their fur is the softest thing I have ever felt and they are the most well behaved little monsters I have ever met."

I laugh even as Devon and Charles groan, "I think we

probably can, we might need to take you to meet their moms though. I think they get final say on who is deemed worthy or a suitable match. Maybe you could come down and train with us sometime soon?"

"I think that would be really fun. So what does Cerberus do that has those two groaning about these sweet babies?"

Later in the evening, after we have all done laughing at stories of Devon and Charles being caught and fetched to my father by an excessively drooling Cerberus, the three of us are heading upstairs when Charles asks, "So, what did you decide on sleeping arrangements?"

"Ah, I had forgotten that you weren't in when I chose my bedroom." I hook my arms in Devon's and Charles', "I chose the master bedroom, it has the most space and I would like you both to be in there regularly. But, as this is all new and we are all still settling into things, I thought it best that you both have your own rooms, and we chose rooms flanking mine. So your room, Charles," I say as we stop before his bedroom door, "is to the left of mine." Devon opens the door to reveal a room decorated in a dark, severe style. Very old world masculine. "While over here," we walk past my door to Devon's and he opens it as well, "on the right is Devon's room." The open door reveals a room decorated in earth tones, warm and inviting. "My room," I say as we walk to the door, "is in the middle. I have set a connecting door for each of you, because I do want you both in here as often as possible." Letting go of their arms I open my bedroom door and flip a light switch as I step in. The two of them follow looking around at the room. "It was all blues but I didn't care for that so I changed it with a wave of my magic hands. If you would like your rooms different, I am happy to do the same for you." They both walk around looking at the enormous suite.

I have a sitting room right as we enter the room, I changed the colors to all dark woods and purples, with silver accents. I mirrored this in the bedroom. I throw open the doors to the actual bedroom, there was an old four post bed frame in the room when I arrived. It was dark and intricately carved, I fell in love with it immediately. They check out my bathroom which has not been altered yet and is a horrifying shade of pepto pink. But it does have a large tub and a separate shower. My walk in closet is amazing and my wardrobe does not do it justice.

Charles comes wandering out of my closet, "Looks like you are going to need to spruce up your wardrobe. You fill a quarter of the thing, if that. Or perhaps Devon and myself could keep some clothing in here as well. For just in case." He says with a grin.

Devon gives him a look I can't decipher. Then he says, "Well, that's all for you tonight Charles," as he puts an arm around his shoulders and guides him over to me, "say goodnight. Then scram. I have plans for her and you had your minute earlier."

Charles chuckles, "I assure you it was longer than a minute." He takes me in his arms and kisses me long and deep, pressing my body into the curve of his. He breaks the kiss and releases me, looking at Devon he says, "There you go, got her all warmed up for you." Then he puts his hands in his pockets and strolls on out the doors to the sitting room, closing them behind himself with a grin.

I can't help but giggle at his antics. Devon however, has other ideas and drawing me to the bed he says, "So, lets see what this bed will stand up to, shall we?"

Nine

FATE

THE NEXT MORNING is a pleasant wake up. Devon in the bed beside me, Charles nearby. Charles sends a messages offering to bring coffee and I tell him I would love that. I tell Devon and he says, "I am not putting on pants for him."

I tell him, "That's fine. You should both be unafraid of seeing each other naked, it is bound to happen."

He cuts his eyes at me, "Should I be concerned?"

"Absolutely not. I would never try to talk you into doing something you were uncomfortable with doing. What I mean is that with the two of you having your own entrances, the probability of you seeing each other naked or seeing the other one having sex with me is pretty high. So you should both be comfortable with seeing each other naked."

"Oh. I hadn't thought about that. I guess that is a thing pretty likely to happen."

Charles walks in then, a tray of coffees with fixings in his hands. He leaves the doors to the sitting room open but I can see the outer door is closed. Charles is wearing a pair of black silk pajama pants and nothing else. He brings a cup to Devon, "I know you prefer your coffee black. Here you go." Then he sets the tray down on the table at the foot of the bed, adding cream and sugar to the other two cups. He walks with those to the other side of the bed, hands me my cup and then setting his cup on the nightstand, crawls into the bed next to me.

Settling himself he leans over and gets his cup of coffee saying, "Ah that's better. No reason for me to drink coffee alone when the two of you are right here. Maria said to tell you that she is making pancakes this morning and you should eat before you train. She also said they would be fortified?"

"Fortified means that she mixes blood in for the vampires." Devon says as I am sipping my coffee, "She keeps the stacks separate, the shifters don't mind it but also don't need it. And they say it makes them smell weird. Maria took that under advisement and made them so you can't smell it but we still get the nourishment."

Charles lays his head on my shoulder, "That is marvelous. I love the innovative spirit she has. So, can I make plans to have my wicked way with you tonight? Claim my turn as it were?"

I can't help but laugh and even Devon chuckles. I tell him, "Yes, you can reserve your time for tonight."

Devon chuckles some more as he adds, "Guess that means I get to corner you in a room this afternoon."

After breakfast I check in with Memré and Natasha making sure that they have everything handled and letting them know that I warded the place so that the only way anyone can enter is if they open the gate. I remind them that Trust and Kindness are roaming the estate, and they should definitely let them know if the gates are being opened for someone. Otherwise, we are likely to have an incident.

Memré chuckles, "Too bad I can't call my ex to come have a visit."

"That would be a way to be done with him." I laugh as I head back toward the kitchen where Devon and Charles are waiting for me. I stop as I enter the kitchen to admire their forms, clad as they are in form-fitting, drool-repelling gear. They are nearly the same height, but that is where the similarity ends. Devon has this powerful build with some serious brawn to him for all that he is generally the most gentle man I have ever met. Charles on the other hand is more the typical weight-lifter shape, broad shouldered and tapering down to a smaller waist but didn't miss leg day either.

I shake my head and walk into the kitchen, stepping up

between the two of them and putting an arm around each. "Ready to go?"

They each slip an arm around me as they say yes and I blink us to the Underworld.

***

Cerberus runs out to great us, much more excited than he has been my previous two trips. I scratch him saying, "It would be really convenient if you could tell me what you are so excited about. I give you permission to speak to me however you are able if that is what you need. I know you talk to Dad."

"She's here! Your mother is back! She just got back a little while ago, I am so happy!"

My eyes widen as Cerberus speaks in my mind, "Holy shit. Was that really all you needed?"

"Yes. It is rude without permission."

"Could you talk to them too, if they gave you permission? Can Trust and Kindness speak to us that way?"

"Yes, and yes. Are they doing well?"

"They are the best, I feel so grateful to have them with us. Thank you and thank your mates for me please. I am so happy to add them to my family. Gentlemen, you should give Cerberus permission to speak to you, as well as Trust and Kindness when we get home."

They quickly give permission to Cerberus who replies to all of us, *"Yes, yes, now can we go see her? I know she will be overjoyed to see you."* As he dances a bit in excitement.

"Yes, lead the way Sir Cerberus." I say and with a hand in his fur I walk along with him, leaving Charles and Devon to trail behind us.

We walk along through the main cavern past the pools and the training room. Up the stairs and through the ball-room into the family portion of the house. We walk into the common area to find my parents sitting on a couch, just cuddling. It is the best sight ever, then Persephone sees me and jumps up, running over to hug me. Only this isn't the Persephone that was at her mother's home. This Perse-phone is dark and mysterious, her eyes hold the secrets of the universe even as she cries happy tears to see me. Her hugs are like magic, I feel healed, then she makes Charles and Devon crowd into the hug as well saying, "I am so glad you are all together finally. And you are coming into your power, thank the stars!" She releases us, grabbing me by the shoulders, "We need to train you, more and harder. Anything to get you fully activated. You have been using magic as often as possible, correct? Like your father told you?"

"Yes, I use it for everything. I feel a little lazy." I say with a chuckle.

Hades has wandered over and Persephone looks between the two of us, tears flowing down her face again, "I am just so happy to have you both here!" She hugs us both, I feel Devon and Charles wandering off toward the ballroom, I don't blame them. I am sure this is all a lot to take in.

DEVON

Charles and I wander off a little from the happy family reunion. I don't want to intrude and who knows what Charles is thinking. But we wander off to the ballroom and enjoy the view.

Charles looks over at me, "Are you really ok with everything?"

"No." I turn to face him, "I absolutely do not want you or your dick anywhere near Fate. But here we are. So I am working on being ok with it. Fate is more important than my feelings of jealousy. And I would have an easier time of it if you hadn't spent such a long time murdering her. Makes it difficult to trust you won't hurt her now. You know?"

Charles crosses his arms in front of his chest, "I understand. I can't even say that I blame you. I would feel the same in your position and I probably would not be as nice or as accepting as you have been. I don't even know why I was killing her all those years. I never meant to. I was always drawn to her, moth meet flame, but then I would get near her and things got foggy and when the fog cleared she would be dead again. I am not sure what was different this time.

Beyond that I watched her grow up, and was around her a lot more, though no one was aware of it, including her. But the fog that was always in the back of my mind dissipated entirely when I turned her. I don't know if it was her blood that did it or having her that close without letting the fog take over, but it was gone after that. She is safe around me now."

"Hmmph. That's good. I still don't like you a whole lot yet."

"Yes. Fair enough. But as we do have to share Fate, and that is apparently how her mother intended it, I feel like we need to make more effort to get along. I can't say I won't continue to mess with you, but I can say that I will not try to keep you from her or push you away from her or anything like that."

Devon shrugs, "I think, maybe we should work on being friends again. Life in general will be a lot safer for Fate if the two of us can work together as a team, instead of just maintaining a truce. It will be easier for us too. So, I will try not to take your jokes so personally. And you can work on knowing where is too far. Asshole."

Charles laughs, "Yes, indeed. Definitely a failing, my not noticing that I am going too far. Asshole is an inaccurate name for me and I can say that I won't get offended when you call me that. Maybe we can convince Fate to put in a pool table, we can drink and play pool."

"Good news on that front, there is a pool table in the house already. You haven't had time to go exploring but the place is gigantic. I would never have thought to buy something so big but Fate, she hasn't had that family feeling before and now that she has it she is determined to take care of everyone and make sure they are all safe. Have everything they could possibly need. So, when she realized this family was growing out of the space she decided to get a house that would fit an army. She is the most amazing woman. Surprise." Charles chuckles, knowing exactly what I am talking about, "Everyone chose bedrooms all over the place, and we still have a lot left. And a lot of different rooms for entertaining and relaxing, there is a sauna in there. The place is wild and she managed to get that all set up in the middle of being kidnapped. Did she tell you that she knew she wasn't coming home?"

Charles scrunches his face, "What do you mean she knew she wasn't coming home?"

I shrug, "I don't know. But the closer we got to that day the more anxious she was and the more she tried to get me to go ahead and turn her. She had everything set up so that things would keep moving even when she was your prisoner. I felt so guilty for not listening to her. When she told you that she was all that stood between you and all of us, she told the truth. Did you know that Memré can liter- ally drop you into a hole in the ground and then close it up over you? When I told her that we could just dig our way out she said she knew that and what fun would it be to be a fly on the wall when we figured out we had to dig through granite? She is horrifying man. Natasha? Nice looking, professional seeming, never flustered Natasha? She will set your balls on fire. And since she controls the flames, she can make them hurt but not actually damage or damage but never stop burning.

Then we have shifters of all kinds running around as her bodyguards. And they love her, most of them had their own issues but Fate chose them and wow. I think they would eat an entire person so Fate wouldn't be hurt. Maria and her two helpers? She knows a few hundred ways to kill us all with food. She adores Fate and would cheerfully serve death to anyone that made her cry. Did I mention that Memré is a fuckin' hacker? She had you located pretty quickly. But the whole time Fate was saying, no, wait. She said that she had a feeling that this needed to be resolved without force. Then Griselda shows up, wait till you meet her, Griselda shows up saying the same damn thing. Even then, we still would have come and got her but she said no. Wait. Give me a few more days, I know it will be better this way. Trust me. So we did, because we didn't believe her when she said something is going to happen."

Charles runs a hand over his face, "Shit. She told me you all were chomping at the bit but that was right before I brought her home and honestly, that wasn't really what she led with. She told me she needed to be with her family. That was her focus, she was good with having me around but she needed her family and you too. Honestly, I was trying to convince her to forget about you. She dismissed the idea entirely. She never denied wanting me but she refused to do anything more than admit to it without being back with you. I didn't tell her but I kind of admired her loyalty. It made me wish she would be loyal to me like that too. Even if I had to share her with you." He snorts, "I minded the idea of sharing with you even less once my father revealed that he was the reason my mother was killed."

"You mean Pru?"

"Ugh… I mean, I can't deny that in a past life she was my mother but, she is nothing like Gretchen was then. I woke up one morning to her kneeling beside my bed, staring at me. I was naked. She didn't want to leave! It still gives me nightmares. And then! Then I get her out of there so I can have a shower, she comes right back in and is holding my towel when I am ready to get out of the shower." Charles shivers and moves to lean against a wall.

I swallow, tugging at a collar that suddenly feels too tight, "I… You have my sympathies. That sounds horrible."

"It was, and she kept calling me her boy and there is just so much to unpack there. Oddly enough, she hates you for being with Fate, but was not willing to have you blamed for her own death in a past life. She nailed my father squarely for that one. Did I tell you he showed up the same day she did? She tried to kill him. And then showed up to spy on our meeting later." Charles chuckles as he rubs his temples, "I had a nice quiet life, drug lord is a good existence when you are hard to kill. After the first twenty years or so, my life was quiet. People didn't really come bothering me because I had a reputation for murdering annoyances. It was not undeserved. Then I decide I can't live without Fate and my whole life blows up around me. Ah well, look at us now. Getting along and talking about our problems."

"Hmmph, I guess. This is not how I pictured things going that's for sure. But I guess in our wildest dreams, none of us would have imagined Fate was the daughter of gods and we had been following her around since her first birth while we were spirits in the Underworld."

Charles nods as we hear them coming down the hall toward us. Hades enters first, "Hello Cretins, are you ready for training today? My gracious queen has decided to teach my amazing daughter all her dirty tricks leaving me time to focus on making sure you are worthy of her. Hope you got lots of bonding time in, we are focusing on teamwork today."

I look at Charles and he looks at me, we shrug and say, "Let's go."

MEMRÉ

Natasha and I are working in the dining room today, it is the only place with a table big enough for us to spread out. The foundation that Fate has planned is going to require a lot of computers and more security than I usually deal with installing. But the magic world has at least as many shady fucks as the mundane. So the code has to be on point and so does the magic.

Between us, we have to decide on a recognition point

for the magic that will mesh with the code and be able to be used for those in the community that are not actually able to do magic though they are magic.

Malachi comes wandering in and sits down as we a discussing this, listening in with no pretense of being there for any other reason. Natasha seems content to ignore him but I am not. I don't know what kind of information he might accidentally or purposely pass on to the wrong parties. "Excuse me a minute Natasha." I turn to face him, "Can we help you?"

"No, I do not require assistance at this time. But I will remember the offer later should I need aid then."

"Ok, since you have decided to pretend at being obtuse, we will dispense with the niceties. Get out. None of this is meant for just anyone to hear. That is why everyone else is staying away. Scram." I point toward the door in case he needs help finding it.

Natasha's eyes go round as Malachi stands with a dark look on his face. She rushes over to him and takes his arm speaking quietly to him. I can't hear exactly what they are saying but I tapped into my powers as soon as his face changed. Natasha stops talking and steps back from Malachi.

His gaze returns to me, "My apologies. I had hoped to get to know you better by watching you at work. Perhaps I will see you at dinner." He turns around and leaves through the door he entered, good goddess what a fine picture that man makes. If only he wasn't such an asshole I might be interested.

Natasha walks back over, sets her hands on the table and sighs, "Girl, you cannot drop an elder vampire into a pit for lacking manners. I agree, he needs to be better but he is and elder and we can't leave him in a cave. Especially since he had no idea that you could do that. He was going to tell you off for not tolerating him in here." Lifting her head to look at me she says, "He is from another time. Yes he has managed ok with all the tech stuff as far as we can see but he puts on a front for everyone. Dammit, I wish Fate was here for her ability to make a conversation private. Look, just know he isn't as comfortable with everything as he seems. Plus, he has been damn near venerated by most that know who he is. Now, in the space of twenty-four hours roughly, he has been thoroughly put back in his place by two different women. Admittedly, Fate is technically a goddess but she doesn't advertise it so he wouldn't know. You don't have to be nice to him or tolerate any crap, but maybe more aware? As in don't jump immediately to dropping him in a pit or telling him off. Can you do that for me? He is important to Billy and Seamus and Ryna. It will hurt all of them if you drop him in a pit."

I throw myself down in a chair, "He is really having trouble with the tech stuff?" I ask as I straighten some papers on the table in front of me.

"Yes. Really. He spends most of his time in the middle of nowhere. That's why it took so long for them to get in touch with him. He is really out of his league here, please give him a break."

"All right. I guess I could maybe try to be nicer to him. I might be a little extra toward him because I am more than a little attracted to him and I don't want to be."

Natasha cocks her head to one side, "Is it because it is him or do you just not want to be attracted to anyone?"

"Anyone. I don't want to get hurt like that again. It killed me when I had to turn in my husband. I don't regret it, he deserves to rot in prison. But I feel like maybe I am flawed. How did I not see what kind of person he was before we got married? Before we had a child together? How could I have missed that? Am I just attracted to the really messed up ones?"

Natasha walks around the table to sit in the chair next to me, "No honey. You aren't messed up or attracted to the really messed up ones. The really messed up ones are just really good at pretending and fooling people. Especially the good people like you." She reaches over and takes my hand, "None of that was your fault and who knows how many you saved by turning him in. You did what many people would or could not. That is what you need to hold onto. Good grief, I thought you were asexual. All this time, we never set you up with anyone because we just thought you were not interested. I wish we had asked. I am so sorry we didn't look any deeper."

I give her hand a squeeze, "Ah, you were just trying to be good friends."

"We were. But that is no excuse for not checking in. Now that I know, I will say, it wouldn't hurt to take a lover. You know you don't have to keep them, right? You could just borrow them for a while. And, Malachi seems pretty interested in you. Maybe borrow him. He is likely to leave eventually, might be a great way to break the ice. If I understand correctly, he doesn't date much either. You two could explore together. Could be the beginning of a beautiful friendship."

I laugh, "I don't think friends often have sex."

Natasha shrugs, "Depends on the friend."

Ten

PRU

I MADE it to the place the voice directed me to, and found the keys to get in exactly where they said they would be. I asked the voice who they were; I know the voice is not my own, I have never been here. They told me all would be revealed in due time.

I did learn a valuable lesson not to sass voices in my head. They have no patience for it and the retaliation hurts. The cottage is empty though I can smell that humans have been here recently. The smell doesn't saturate the place so I don't think they live here. Going inside I look around, it is a boring little cottage in a boring little forest. I spot the kitchen and wander in, I haven't had a bite since I left Charles' place. Opening the fridge I see it is barely stocked and no blood to be had. There is some meat in the freezer, but frozen meat won't have much blood in it. I am contemplating what to do for food when it walks in.

I hear them step inside after unlocking a door that wasn't locked to begin with, they call out, "Hello? I was told to bring by some supplies." They walk into the kitchen and I see it is a man, he looks delicious. "Oh, hi! The owner said they had a friend coming to stay here and they asked me to drop some things by." He switches all the bags to one hand and sticks out the now free hand, "My name is Chad."

I smile at Chad as I take his hand, "Hi Chad, so nice to meet you, I am Pru. I just got here, what goodies have you brought me?"

He sets his bags on the counter and begins unpacking them, excitedly detailing all the items he brought. I sidle up close to him, pressing up against his side. His heart starts to beat faster and his breathing becomes quick, shallow. He turns to me like he would say something but I stretch up on my tiptoes to kiss his lovely mouth. He dives into the kiss, quick and easy. I remember how long it has been since I have had a man. I wrap my arms around his neck as he turns to press more of his body against me.

The kisses aren't enough, I need more friction. Working at the buttons on his shirt I quickly have it opened, his chest revealed to my greedy hands. He moans and breaks the kiss, "I don't have any protection."

"I haven't been with anyone in over ten years. No disease here and I will pick up a morning after pill tomorrow." I lean in and take his nipple in my mouth, sucking hard.

He sucks air through his teeth, "I haven't been with anyone since my wife left me, almost a year ago, aaaaahh-hh…." His sentences trails off as I get his jeans opened and kneel in front of him, taking him in my hot mouth. I feel his cock twitching as he clutches the edge of the counter crying out, "I, I can't hold on. It's been too long, oh god, oh, I am going to cum if you don't stop… aaaahhh."

I slowly withdraw his cock from my mouth, giving the head one final lick, causing his breath to hitch just as he had started to breathe again. I stand in front of him, his eyes are closed and his breathing still a bit ragged. I strip off all my clothes while he tries to control himself. He opens his eyes to find me naked in front of him. Determination in his eyes he steps out of his jeans while telling me, "I have never cum before a woman in my life and I'm not going to start now, get on that counter."

I hop up on the counter as he gets on his knees in front of me. He buries his face in my pussy and it is like being worshipped. His tongue working my clit in a way that I have never experienced has me nearly over the edge, then he slides a finger into me and I scream as the orgasm rips through my body. He keeps up his ministrations until I start to pull away from the sensation overload.

He stands with a smile on his face, wiping away the evidence of my pleasure. "Now, would you like to try for another?"

I look at him in surprise, "You want to make me cum again?"

"Gods yes! I am not a one hit wonder. Are you game?"

"Yes! I have to warn you, I might bite."

"You'll have to save the biting for after." He opens a cabinet, pulls out a folding step stool and sets it on the floor under where my feet dangle. He tugs me off the counter, bracing the stool with a foot on either side till I am standing on it. He pushes lightly on my back, whispering, "Lean over the counter." I do as he says and he rubs his cock between my dripping lips. The contact is amazing and I feel my core clenching in anticipation. I hold still as he slowly slides his cock into my entrance, it feels like I might die from the pressure of his cock filling me and what a way to go. When it feels like I will break from the stretch his thighs touch my ass. He holds himself so very still saying, "Oh gods, oh, don't move. You are so hot and wet and so fucking tight. I need. Minute, I need a minute. Oh sweet Jeeves, this is the best pussy I have ever been in, just, just a little longer. Oh man, you make me so hard, I want to feel you cum on my cock."

His stream of sexy talk is just making me hotter, I want him to touch me, fuck me already. The feel of his shaft inside me is glorious and I just want him to pound the orgasm out of me. I feel him lean forward over me and then his fingers are rubbing my clit in slow circles as he withdraws, I moan as the sensations. He takes his hand from my clit and I whimper, then his hand is on mine as he whispers in my ear, "Touch yourself while I fuck you."

And he guides my fingers to the slow circles he was making on my clit.

It's only the head in when he straightens and places a hand on each hip. He pushes back in slowly, I can feel him watching as my hand works faster and faster. He hits bottom and reverses, still going so slow.

I groan, "Ah gods Chad, fuck me hard! I need it now!"

His hands grip my hips tighter and then he slams into me over and over. My mind spins out of control as he pounds the orgasm out of both of us. Moments later he is leaned over me, his hands braced on the counter as he gasps for air. I am no better off, the fireworks still going off in my core have my head laid on the coolness of the countertop.

"Good Gods Chad, why did your wife leave you?Are you abusive or mean? Did you learn these tricks after? That's got to be it. You couldn't have been doing this and she still left you."

He chuckles as he pulls himself out of me. He grabs a paper towel from the nearby roll, holding it on himself he walks over to grab a dishtowel and brings that back to me as I step off the stool and turn around to lean back on the counter. I may be a vampire, but the first two orgasms in ten plus years have me feeling like jello. I take the towel from him and he turns his own attention to his clean up and throwing away his paper towel while I swipe through a couple times to get the worst of it.

"Where is the bathroom in this place? The kitchen is as far as I got before you arrived."

He points across the living room to a hallway just visible from where I stand. "First door on the right." I scoop up my clothes and head that way. I listen to him moving around in the kitchen as I clean up and dress. I am a little surprised he is still here. I also don't know quite what to do with him now.

I exit the bathroom, leaving the dish towel hangin over the edge of the tub. Heading back to the kitchen I watch his throat work as he downs a glass of water. Pulling the glass away he sucks air again and says, "So, really nice to meet you. Um, I don't want to pressure you but I think I might like to get to know you, maybe try to repeat that experience? If you wanted that. I can go home an never darken your door again if you prefer that, and no hard feelings. Well, maybe some hardness but only every time I think about the mind blowing sex. What I mean is that I won't be upset. Yes, that's it. No upset, plenty of hard going to happen when I think back on this."

I smile at him, "I think I would like for you to stay but I am not sure when my friend is going to arrive… I don't know how she will feel about that?"

"I have it on good authority that she won't be here for at least four days. That's why she asked me to bring over the groceries, to tide you over till she got here with more."

"Then I would really like for you to stay. Do you have any steaks in the supplies? I find I am really hungry for a bloody, rare steak."

He laughs, "I think your friend knew you might want steaks, she specified them. Said they might save my life. I loaded you up on steaks. Would you like me to cook or would you prefer to do it?"

"You cook too? Ok, I know this is really personal, but why did your wife leave you? I feel like I should be worried about you being a serial killer or something."

He looks away, "I did get violent. Not with her, but with the guy she was seeing. She started seeing a guy at work behind my back. I knew something was up when she stopped wanting to have sex with me. Eventually I started prying. Watching and noticing things. I figured out who he was and for some reason I thought killing him would bring her back. As it turns out, that is not how it works."

I am stunned, he is just perfect. I might have to keep this guy.

"Well, I guess you probably are ready for me to get out now." He says as he collects his keys and starts to walk past me head down.

I grabs his arm as he walks in front of me, "Where do you think you are going?"

He looks down at my hand in surprise, "I thought you would want me to leave?"

"Oh no. Not at all. You are not the only one with murderous tendencies here. I will tell you my secret and then you can decide if you stay or go. But you have to promise never to reveal my secret or I will have to hunt you down and kill you."

His eyes widen at that last bit, "Um, sure. I mean, yes. I can keep your secret. I mean, most people don't know that it wasn't a psychotic break that caused me to kill him, so you have my secret too. I'll keep yours if you keep mine."

He leans against a counter and folds his arms across his chest, waiting patiently. I swallow, I haven't told any humans about this. Oh well, deep end here I come. "I am a vampire. I drink blood regularly to survive and I have killed a couple people in relation to that."

"I thought you were going to tell me a real secret. This is not cool. Not cool at all Pru."

"Wait, Chad. What if I could prove it to you?"

"How would you prove it to me?"

"I can bite you, on the arm or something, so you can see my teeth as they… didn't realize that would be a turn on…"

He smiles, "I mean, why not? Before you do, you aren't going to kill me are you? I would like to have sex at least once more before I die. So if you could hold off on the making me dead, that would be great."

I grin at him, "No worries lover boy. I want a repeat performance too. Let me have your arm."

He holds his arm out and I stay on the outside of his arm, in case he wants to jerk his arm away I don't want him pulling me in towards him when all he wants is me away. I run my fingers down his arm and I watch the goose bumps raise on him as my teeth elongate. I open my mouth wider than I usually would and look up to watch his face as I lower my mouth to his arm. He is watching me, utterly focused on the descent of my mouth to his arm. He doesn't look frightened though. His mouth is open a little, pupils dilated, his breathing fast like his heart rate. My fangs pierce his skin, his eyes roll up in his head. A moan escapes his lips as I drink lightly from him. His blood tastes so good and he is really enjoying this. His eyes are closed now, his head thrown back. I don't want him weak so I cut myself off long before I want to, licking the wounds to heal them.

"Ah gods, why did you stop? That felt so good. I thought it would hurt at least a little. But no. I see how you are able to feed off people and they just stay put." His whole body shivers and he straightens, opening his eyes to look at me. "Can you maybe feed a little more later when we have sex again? I feel like that might be…" He shudders again.

I smile at him, biting my lip, "I would really like that. But first, steaks. I don't want to do that a second time while I am this hungry. You taste really good and I feel like it might be detrimental to your health."

AJAH

I am due downstairs with the rest of the bodyguards in the next five minutes. John, Brad, and Steve are waiting at the door to the new workout room. Owen is somewhere in the house, but no idea where that might be. John was doing door duty, but I got Benny to cover for him. Ok, if I were a bear, where would I want to be to relax? Movie room? I'll check the kitchen on my way to the movie room. That is the hungriest guy I have ever met.

I spot him leaving the kitchen as I come down the hall, "Owen!"

He turns around with a whole turkey leg in his hand, "Mmmpphh ydoufwe noun mhouhe?"

"My dude, you have got to finish chewing before you try to talk. Eat fast. We need to get to the training room, Ryna said she has a new set up she wants us to run through.

We get to the door where the others are waiting and Steve hands me a note, "This was slipped under the door a few minutes ago." He hands the note over and starts to limber up like the others are doing.

I raise a brow at him and open the note:

I don't rely on scent enough and shifters use it too much. Today's challenge is based on that flaw in our hunting styles. Your task today is to find me as I move through the room, while not getting caught by Trust and Kindness. They will be hunting you while you hunt me.

Don't worry, Trust and Kindness have assured me that no one has ever actually drowned in drool.

I crumble the note, "Sorry guys. Looks like this one is my fault. I was the one that told her she isn't using her sense of smell enough."

Owen finishes his turkey leg, "No worries Ajah. If we

couldn't handle a lot of smells and something hunting us while we hunt something else what good would we be as bodyguards? This ought to be a great challenge!" With that a ripple runs over him. Fur sprouts following the ripple and he changes shape, going from bipedal human to bear. He is flipping humongous. The hall is suddenly a lot smaller.

"John, can you open the door for him? We can follow Sir Bear in and maybe they will be distracted with him."

"Yeah, got it."

Owen jumps through the door, mostly. He gets stuck midway. "Hang on Owen, we'll give you a shove to get you through." I say as we all laugh at how he stopped mid-leap like that. The four of us line up behind him and once everyone get a handful of bear ass we all give him a push. He moves an inch forward and then this loud, long fart blasts John in the face. I collapse laughing as John starts choking and coughing. Steve and Brad are just as incapacitated as I am, helpless on the floor while John dry heaves. Owen, considerably less bloated slips on through the door but turns around to look back at us. I call out to Ryna and the hounds, "Hold! We had problems getting in the room! Hold till we can get up! John is sick!"

Moments later Ryna lands lightly next to Owen. She gives him a pat and looks in the door at John on the floor still clutching his stomach and then turns to me, tears streaming down my face and also clutching my stomach but in laughter. "What happened to John?"

John recovers himself at that point, "That fucking bear!

That fucking bear ate something dead too long! Fucking carrion eater! Jaysus Krispies! I have never smelled something from another creature that put me down like that! Fucking shit!"

I sit up, wiping away the tears, "So Owen got stuck in the door when he tried to leap on through. We all got behind him to give him a push. We pushed and he slid an inch or so and then…" laughter is bubbling up again despite my best efforts and getting the rest is beyond me but John manages.

"That fucking bear farted in my gawd-damned face! That's what she is trying to say! The fucking bear made me dry-heave with his gas in my fucking face!"

Ryna's lips are twitching like mad as she excuses herself saying that they would wait until we had all collected ourselves and made it in the room, closing the door is the signal that we are ready. I wave her on as I wipe tears from my eyes again.

Some minutes later we make it into the room and close the door. The lights immediately go out, not that big a deal because we can all see better than most at night. Then the smells are released. It is like a miasma of scent. None of it seems to come from any one place. It is everything and nothing individual.

John says, "This is better than what came out of Owen, I can live with it. Just makes it a challenge to find her. Still possible."

To our right and left we hear growling. "Ah hell, the

hounds are ready to play!" I say as I sprint into a pathway, trying to avoid being bathed in drool.

By the end of the training period we have all been drooled on by the dogs. Owen lays claim to having gotten the worst of it. He turned bear when this started so he was too big to be picked up when Trust and Kindness caught him, without sizing themselves beyond what the room could allow. Since they have ideas about fair play they licked him, a lot. His fur is dripping with it, none of us quite sure how he is going to get that out of his fur. Or get through the house without tracking drool the entire way. Ryna went and got us all towels to clean up the worst on ourselves and she works to get Owen clean enough to walk through the house without leaving puddles. He is massive so she is still working on him when we finish toweling ourselves down. The sad bear noises Owen has been making the whole time have convinced everyone but John to help get him dried enough to get out of the house to be hosed down. After that he can lay in the sun to bake dry.

John just throws his towel at Owen, "Serves you right ya smelly bastard." Owen makes a sad sound that reminds me of Chewbacca, and John retorts, "I don't want to hear it. You can be a big guy and eat to maintain it without putting your gut, and me, through what you are doing to it. Take some probiotics or something."

With that he stomps out of the room. We all laugh and

Ryna pats Owen's leg, "Don't worry, he'll be over it by tomorrow. I wouldn't take it personal either. John is probably got other problems that had him salty before you happened to him."

"Yeah, he is plain cranky today. He will likely come talk to you tomorrow," Steve says as he picks up John's towel, "but in the meantime, I think if we play this training game again maybe don't go bear for the event? Trust and Kindness are very thorough and well, drool is much easier to clean off skin than fur. Come on, I'll open doors for you and hose you off outside. Good thing it's a sunny day."

We all step back and Owen ambles out behind Steve who says, "I'll drop these in the laundry on my way out."

The rest of us look around, realizing we have to clean up the mess left on the floor too. Brad sighs, "I'll get the mop and bucket while you two work on wiping up what you can."

<hr>

PRU

The days I have spent with Chad are the best I have ever had. But today is the day the voice in my head is due to arrive so he has gone home, though he left me his number and directions to his home. He didn't want to leave, but I feel like it might be safer for him to not be here when she arrives. I clean the house from top to bottom while I wait. I may be feeling mellow again but I have the feeling that my voice is probably still angry, if the way she sounded and had me feeling on the way out of Charles' place is any indication.

It is strange how the anger I have always felt toward Fate seems to have dissipated since the voice isn't speaking to me. Like I remember being mad at her and I remember why, but it doesn't seem like I should have been mad at her to begin with. And that voice in my head, the more I think about it the more I feel like I have heard it somewhere before, I just don't know where I heard it before.

She arrives late afternoon. Just pops into the living room, no fanfare or even the noise of a vehicle. I am in the kitchen when she arrives and I see her pop in. She looks odd. Her manner of dress, body type, and features all say earth mother type. But her eyes, movements, and demeanor all say deeply unhappy, destroyer of all things good.

What have I gotten myself into?

She looks around and spots me, "Oh good, you haven't run off somewhere. Come, sit with me and we will discuss what you are going to do for me."

"Your voice sounds so familiar. Have we met before?"

"Oh yes. We have. You parents were devotees of mine," She sits in a chair, "I am Demeter."

"Demeter? Goddess of harvest and seasons? Mother of Persephone and some others we never heard a whole lot about?"

"Yes. That one. Your parents were devotees to me, I

often spoke to them through a particular crystal I gifted them for the purpose. I blessed you as mine when you were a tiny thing, to keep you from coming to harm by your sister. She is what I need your help with."

"I don't know how much help I will be. Last time I went up against her I ended up where you found me, drugged into a comatose state." Just saying it I remember the warm darkness and how peaceful it was, the nice woman that came to soothe all the places that hurt. Such a nice place. Maybe…

"Exactly! Because she is half demon spawn. She must be stopped and then her body must be brought to me so that I can lay her to rest permanently. Her demon half must not succeed in its plan to gain control of enough power to usurp the very gods themselves."

"Why would she do that?"

"Because dear, that is what demons do, they seek out power and then use it to become the supreme ruler. The only way to separate her soul from her demon side is to kill her and bring me her body, my angel Baal knows the ceremony to sunder the ties the demon side of her uses to bind itself to her soul."

"You are working with an angel? I thought they were forbidden to even acknowledge other—"

"Yes, yes, tiresome. Special case and all that. Which is why I need you to collect her body for me. I can't do it for reasons beyond your comprehension. It must happen soon or her demon will be too strong for us to take on. I will help you as much as I can. First, come kneel before me, let's see if I can restore your magic."

I could have my magic back? I near leap over to kneel in front of her. Demeter places a hand on either side of my head and I feel a warm energy followed by pain! The pain racks through my body, but I can't move away. The pain grows with every second and I can hear the screams of the damned ringing in my ears.

I wake up on the floor. Demeter in the kitchen cooking. I feel like a bus ran me over. A lot. "What happened? Did it work?"

Demeter sighs, "No. Sadly my daughter is in on this and one god cannot remove the work of another. I do have good news, when Fate dies, so will her spell. All you have to do is make sure she dies; you get your magic back and Baal gets to finish his angelic assignment. Everyone wins. Besides, you want Fate dead anyway, don't you? Hasn't she always been evil? Your parents knew the evil that lurked in her heart. That's why they had you monitoring her."

I feel a sudden rage come over me and I know it is all Fate's fault. Everything, I wouldn't have lost my husband or my baby boy if it wasn't for her. I would have had the love of my parents if not for Fate being there first, poisoning them so all they saw me as was a tool to keep her in line. "You're right. It's all Fate's fault. With her out of the picture everything will be just fine. Just as it always should have been."

The rage clawing at my throat calms, banked and waiting till I see Fate again.

For the last time.

"How is your son? I understand Fate has him in her sway?"

"She does. He fancies himself in love with her. He fawns over her, says I can't kill her."

"Oh. He has been in contact with her?"

"Yes. He held her prisoner at his house. Last I heard he was taking her home and staying there indefinitely to be near her. Makes me sick. He barely had anything to do with me and didn't appreciate any of the things I tried to do for him. It's like she cast a spell on him. That's it! She must have cast a spell on him, something to make him blind to anything but her. Why else would he ignore his mother after all this time?"

Eleven

FATE

TODAY IS A HOME DAY, no training. Of course that only means that I need to tend to a million other things. Like working to get in touch with the next family in line, I still have to hunt down all the things Charlie left secreted all over the city. I need to meet with Natasha and Memré to find out how the foundation set up is coming along. I think we may be at a point where I will need to hire an accountant, set some money off to one side for the foundation and just start to really get things more sorted. But that is a lot of deep thinking for someone who hasn't gotten her first cup of coffee yet this morning.

I sit up and Charles wraps an arm around my waist, snatching me over to him asking, "Is it really time for getting out of bed already?"

"It is," I say as I twist around to snuggle him a little

bit. This is the first night he has gotten to sleep in here with me and I know he is loathe for it to end. "I think that is Devon I hear coming up the stairs with coffee right now."

Devon knocks and opens the door, tray with coffees in one hand. Closing the door behind him he delivers a coffee to Charles. For his part Charles sat up to take the coffee while I scooted over to be more in the middle and sit upright with my legs crossed in front of me. Devon sets the coffee tray down on the nightstand before he slips into the bed. He chose to wear nothing but pajama bottoms in this morning as well, I am not mad about it. His chest and shoulders are magnificent. I watch them as he turns to get our coffees off the tray, I could watch that show a lot longer. Devon has made each coffee as preferred by the recipient and I am impressed. I don't know how he found out the way Charles prefers his but, great job working to make things better between the two of them.

I settle back on my pillows to sip my coffee and ask them, "What are your plans for the day?"

I watch the two look at each other and Devon gesture for Charles to go first, "I need to touch base with my guys, make some phone calls. I may need to step out at some point briefly, but I should be gone no more than a few hours. Business goes on and though I am stepping back some, I still make the major decisions and occasionally remind people that I am still here. Especially the heads of other cartels. They need reminders."

Devon nods as Charles finishes, "That does seem tiresome. I have some things to go over with my accountant, he is going to visit the house. I will be busy most of the day with him but I will be here. What do you have planned?"

I take a sip of my coffee, "Well, I still need to hunt down all the things that Charlie hid. I don't really have time to go all over the city to do it myself, but I do have the ability to glamour other people to appear as me. I think I want to send some of the body guards out to collect those things. Keep a couple of them here just in case and send the rest treasure hunting. I think it would be fun for them and I can give the group bonuses based on what they all bring back. Plus, I need to closet up with Natasha and Memré, go through some things. Maybe hire another person. Definitely need an accountant. So I guess I need to call Maggie and put out the magical job board."

Devon swallows a sip of coffee, "I think sending out the bodyguards with a glamour to look like you is a really great idea, very safe for you. They are all shifters and vampires, so not very likely to be permanently injured and they are used to looking out for attacks."

Charles nods, "I agree, but maybe make them magically bullet proof anyway? No one likes being shot and you do have an assassin out there. My intel suggested that she isn't the kind to give up just because you got away or her employer died of a heart attack. I think you will need to take care of her sooner rather than later."

I shrug, "I guess this could accidentally kill two birds with one stone. If she attacks one of them and they take

her out, one less thing to worry about. I feel sorry for her if
my parents get hold of her and realize who she was trying
to kill."

Charles looks over at me, "How does that work? What
if they were devout Christians? Do they still see your
father as the leather clad Hades, Grim Lord of theUn-
derworld?"

Devon chuckles and I answer, "I asked him a similar
question. He said that they all see different things based on
what they believe and what they deserve. So a good Chris-
tian comes in and sees him as God, goes off to Heaven.
Bad Christians see him as Satan, they go off to the pool to
be cleansed but still see it as writhing in the pits of hell.
Buddhists, Hinduists, etc; they all see him and her based
on their preconceived notions. It is kind of wild." I swig
the last of my coffee, "I suppose I need to shower now. Get
started on the day."

Devon grins, "Want some help?"

Charles looks over at him, "I'll play you for it."

Devon raises a brow while I stand up and head for the
shower saying, "You two decide, I am getting in the
shower."

I hear Charles say, "Rock, paper, scissors."

Devon agrees and I get in the shower, I can wait to find
out who won. My face is turned up to the spray and my
eyes closed when I feel someone come up behind me.
Hands explore my body and I am not sure I care which one
it is. I turn around and wipe my closed eyes free of the
water. Opening them I find Charles standing in front of

me. He grins down at me and grabs my ass in both hands, pulling me against him. "I won, paper covers rock." He picks me up, sliding me along the length of his body until his cock is free to line itself up with my entrance, I wrap my legs around his body and he lowers me, slowly impaling me on his hardness. My eyes roll back and I let my head hang back as I grip his shoulders, digging my nails in.

I feel him take a nipple in his mouth as he lifts me up again. I moan, "Oh gods, just fuck me!"

My nipple released from his mouth he lifts me completely off him and sets me down on my feet. I open my eyes just in time for him to spin me around so I am facing away from him. Then his hands leave my body and I hear him leave the shower. I look around just in time to see him bring the step from my closet into the shower. It is a plastic step but it lets me reach the top shelf. He sets it down in front of me and I can hear Devon laughing from the other room.

I step up on it facing the wall and lean forward a little, bracing my hands on the wall in front of me. He steps up behind me, lining himself up and pushing in just a little. Just enough to get the head seated inside me. Then he puts his hands on my breasts, pinching my nipples hard as he rams his cock into me as far as he can. Still pinioning in and out of me he releases one nipple to reach down and slips his first finger and thumb between my pussy lips, lightly pinching my clit. I nearly cum on him right then.

He says, "So you do like it rough. Good." He twists my

nipple a little, maintaining the pressure of his fingertips, pulling on my clit and leaning forward to bite my shoulder as he slams into me. I cum on his cock right then, waves of pleasure exploding through my body as he fucks me harder while he drinks a little from my shoulder and gets a light show from the flames covering my body.

He pounds into me a few more times before he lets go of my shoulder to yell my name as he buries himself in me, I can feel his seed spilling into me as my pussy clenches around him over and over.

Releasing my clit and nipple he moves his hands to my waist, and thank goodness because my legs are feeling a bit like jello.

We stand there till I regain the full use of my legs and step down from the stool. He pulls me gently around the stool to hold me close, "I love you Fate. Thank you for accepting me as one of your bonded mates."

"I love you too. Now let go, I need to get clean so I can get to work." He laughs as he releases me, I slant a look at him but I do need to get ready so I grab the shampoo and start my routine.

We are quickly finished and out of the shower. He wraps a towel around himself, "I'll see you later." He kisses my lips and strolls out of the bathroom. I finish drying my hair enough that it won't drip and walk out of the bathroom naked to find Devon lounging on the bed, his pajama pants discarded on the floor.

He grins seeing me notice him, "Hey lil goddess, why don't you come over here and let me worship you?"

I feel my lips moving into a smile as I walk over to the bed, "We both need to get to work. Are you sure you want to right after?"

He reaches out and takes my hand tugging me onto the bed, and on top of him. "I told you that I would just have to fuck you better and I meant that." He laughs as he says it, "No, really, it was seriously hot listening to him fuck the hell out of you and now I am left in need. Help a guy out?"

He reaches up to caress my breasts, flipping his thumbs across my still sensitized nipples, I suck air through my teeth and my hips rock forward a little, dragging my still wet lips across his cock. He groans and presses up with his hips, his shaft slipping between my lips to press on my clit. I can't say no to that and I lean forward, reaching a hand behind myself to line him up as I slowly slide onto his cock. His moans turn me on and I tease him, rolling my hips as I move up and down on him, his greedy eyes trying to stay open even as they roll back and another moan escapes his lips.

Swirling my way down his cock I stop with him as far in as I can get him and start to grind back and forth on him, only withdrawing him a half inch or so as my core clenches around him. I know it will be minutes before I cum again, "Oh goddess, I'm nearly there! Cum with me Devon!"

He grabs my hips and starts pounding in and out of me, I fall right over the edge of the cliff screaming, "Devon!" as I cum on him, the brightness of my flames illuminating the room while I feel him slam into me a few more times and he joins me. I lean over him, lowering my chest to rest on his as his arms come around me.

"I love you Fate."

"I love you my sweet Devon. I want to try something tonight. If you are okay with it?"

His hands making slow circles on my back he asks, "What's that?"

"I would like to try sleeping tonight with both of you cuddling with me. Just sleeping. I am not trying to push you two into that, and if you aren't comfortable with this, I won't bring it up again. But I love hanging out with the two of you in the mornings. I would skip coffee in bed just to spend the first part of the morning with the two of you."

"I can't say yes for certain, because I would need to talk with Charles, but I think he might be ok with that. If he is, then I am."

I sit up, "Really? You will?"

"I will. If Charles is ok with it." He smacks my ass, "Now let me up vixen, we need to work."

I laugh and lean down to kiss him one more time. Lifting up off of him I head to the bathroom so I can clean up again…

I head downstairs and see John, "Hey, could you collect all the bodyguards? And anyone else interested in some treasure hunting?"

He grins, rubbing his hands together, "I sure can. Where do you want us?"

"Kitchen please, I am on my way there now."

He is gone like a flash as I continue to the kitchen. I think having them work on the treasure hunt will be a good diversion for them all. Maria hands me a cup of coffee as soon as I walk in the kitchen. Thanking her I sit at the island, Trust and Kindness join me, I turn so I can scratch both of them as they relate the events of the past few days. I giggle a bit over the training that has been happening, as it closely mirrors what Hades uses to put Devon and Charles through their paces. Except for the farting, I don't think he has bears farting. I don't know if I should tell him about that or not, I don't think the guys would thank me for it.

All the bodyguards plus Ryna and Seamus enter the kitchen. They are all joking with each other and I love listening to it. Trust and Kindness wander over to mingle with everyone and get more scratches, so I sip my coffee and enjoy the warmth. In the corner of the kitchen I notice our resident ghost, so I give her a nod. She puts her hands over her heart and offers a watery smile before she fades away.

I realize as she does that, everyone is watching me. "What? Did I sprout a horn?"

Seamus speaks up from the far side of the crowd, "Well, you were having a moment and we were just trying to figure out with whom?"

"Oh! I guess that did look odd. The ghost was really

happy having all this life in her house and I was agreeing with her. We have created the best found family a girl could ever hope to have. I feel really blessed to have you all in my life."

"Aw," John says, "That's great. Keep it to yourself. Now about that treasure…"

Owen nudges him with an elbow, shaking his head no when John turns to look at him. John shrugs and they all turn to me, waiting.

"Well, I suddenly don't have the time or the safety to go hunting all the things that Charlies secreted around the city. I was hoping that I could talk you all into working on it for me? I would create glamours for each of you, I can put it on a pin. That way you can carry it in a pocket till you need it. Or you can put it on and wander about as me. Could be entertaining for you. Just to be clear, you will be wandering about as the old me. Plain, pale, and glasses wearing me. There may well be other people looking to collect on the bounty Charlie paid to the one assassin I know of, or maybe he paid more than one. Who knows? There are so many things I didn't know about him while we were together. I would also shield you, so that any projectiles hitting you would still make an impact, but it would be greatly lessened and nothing would be able to pierce your body."

Seamus is first to answer, "Sounds fun. I've always wanted to know what it was like walking the world as a white woman. Can you dress me pretty?"

I laugh, "Yes, we can do that if you want. Anyone else?"

Everyone agrees, and they decide to check with Charles' guys, see if one of them would go to even the teams. Benny agrees, and I get started creating pins. I make four total, each one needing skin contact to be active. Seamus's I make so it is dressed nice, since he requested it. Afterwards, I spent some time shielding everyone. The shields I placed are strong enough to keep them whole and un-crushed even with an explosion. They will still hurt, but they will have plausible damage, bruises and such in case of humans getting to them.

That done I hold out my hand and make the box of videos Charlie made appear in my hand. I hand them over, "These contain all the directions he left his girlfriend on how to find everything. Probably should watch out for her too. She looks very similar to me, her name is Amalia. Oh, I almost forgot!" I wave one hand over the other and four temporarily existing ID cards appear in my hand. Handing them out I tell them, "These have a day shelf life. By sunrise tomorrow, they will disappear into the ether. Beyond that, take notes on the videos and happy hunting!"

They all disperse to watch the video and Maria, she brings me an omelet that smells so good I could cry. I thank her profusely and she glows. I love that she is happy working here and that this is a good place for her. The very last thing I would want would be for her to feel over-worked or under-paid. Come to think of it…. "Hey Maria, do you need more help? I know you have two helpers, but this is a lot of house. You are the overseer and chef here, so if you want or need more help, we will get that for you."

Maria looks wide-eyed for a moment, "I didn't want to say anything. I feel so very lucky to have this job. I didn't want to mess anything up."

That answer makes me suspicious that she has other concerns. Someone as talented as she is could work for any number of people. "Maria, you can't mess this up by asking for enough people to do the job properly. Is there another concern? Do you not have a green card?"

Maria pales as the sentence leaves my mouth. I can smell the terror coming off her, I cross the room to hug her, "Maria, you don't ever have to worry that we will use that against you. If you want to apply for one we will support you in that." I release her and step back, "If you don't, we will support you in that. Our support is not contingent on you not making waves. If we act like lazy pendejos, you tell us. If you need more help, let us know. And if la migra pick you up, you just keep calling my name. Doesn't have to be loud, you can whisper it. I will hear you. I will absolutely come for you. If you decide you just want an American identity created for you, I feel pretty certain Charles has contacts for that, or come to think of it, probably all the vampires do. You are family now, we take care of family. Now, do you want to choose the people or do you want me to get Maggie to send over some people?"

Maria sniffs once, "Get over there and eat that omelet.

Don't you let my good food go to waste. Shoo!" I smile and walk back to the island, "As for the people, I will find them. I know people that are honest and need a good place to work. I will bring them to meet you, If you approve, they will start working." She turns back to the stove, "As for the other, I never—" she stops and clears her throat, "I never imagined those things possible. I didn't cross legally, I flew over the border as an owl. I don't know what I want. Do you mind if I think about it?"

"You take as long as you need. We aren't going anywhere. And you have full authority to hire whoever you need or want working here. You are the overseer so to speak, I want to be kept in the loop but beyond that, you have to deal with them and your standards are even higher than mine."

Maria nods and keeps her back toward me as she moves about. I feel like she might like some time to herself so I finish my food as quickly as possible and deposit my dishes in the dishwasher.

I tell Maria thanks for the excellent breakfast as I head off to find Natasha and Memré.

I find them in the formal dining room, Papers spread across the table and deep in discussion about the foundation and what OS they should use. Natasha is hard for the Windows OS while Memré wants anything else. They both look to me as I walk in saying in unison, "Pick one."

I have no idea what is better so I ask Natasha, "Why do you think we should use Windows?"

She lists the reasons, ticking each off on a finger, "Ease of use, most people already know the Windows system to some extent, cost, and all the programs I know are already set for Windows while they may or may not be set for anything else. Learning a new operating system is a pain, or so I have heard because admittedly I haven't used any other system."

"Okay… Memré, why do you want anything other than Windows and what is your preferred system? And why?" I ask as I sit down at the table, I have heard Memré talk about OS's before, I know I want to be seated for this. I am also pretty sure I want to go with whatever Memré suggests because she knows more about these things than Natasha or myself.

"First, Windows is the most hacked operating system there is. The additional cost of virus protection is ridiculous, especially since most of the ways for hackers to get in are backdoors created by Windows so that they can get into the OS. You could go online right now and find three hacked versions of Windows without even trying hard. Second, if we are going to have information about magical creatures on here, do you really want a system that has all those well used backdoors built in? Doors that are wide open for anyone with enough money and the desire to use the magical community to their benefit?" I watch Memré pace as she rants, she really is exceedingly knowledgeable about these things and Natasha pales over some of the things she lists as reasons not to use Windows.

I finally cut her off, "Memré, what is your OS preference?"

"Linux. I would create such a system…" She sighs, "But that isn't practical here because it won't necessarily work with all or even most of the software that Natasha and you will need. So, Mac. Their OS is popular enough that the vast majority of programs have been made compatible, and the few that are not," she shrugs, "have alternatives that often end up being better than the original they are replacing. The need for virus protection is non-existent and with a vpn, we can secure things better than the average. I can set a magical link checker, so that we don't need to worry about anyone storing the data from the links they check for us. Or storing data when they sift through things looking for the links to check. Plus, with the changes Windows has made to be competitive with Mac, the learning curve isn't what it used to be. Honestly, the worst part is that the scrolling is reversed."

I look over at Natasha, she nods while Memré isn't looking. I thought perhaps she was protesting because she hadn't heard Memré, hadn't let her explain why even though she is our resident computer expert. Natasha doesn't really like computers and the idea of learning a new OS would be intimidating for her. "I guess that settles it. Natasha, we have to go with the Mac OS." She looks relieved right up until I say, "Memré you will go through with each of us that are going to be working within the foundation and ascertain what programs we need, our level of ability with the system and help us where we need it?"

Memré looks at me like I have grown a second head as she knows I am familiar with Mac. I cut my eyes toward Natasha who is, thankfully, engrossed in a message on her phone. Memré catches on immediately and says, "Oh, yes. Of course. I wouldn't dream of turning you two out into the wilds of the Mac OS without some knowledge."

After that the conversation moved on and we discussed the dire need for an accountant. Natasha made a note to call Maggie and see if we knew an accountant in the magical community, barring that we decided that we could check in with the rest of the vampires, mostly they had sizable estates that were managed by human accounting firms. We were all agreed on not using Devon's accountant and on talking him into switching. He was obviously not the most reliable of people as Charles had only paid him a little to call Devon and set him up. It made me wonder if Devon's money was really safe with him.

Malachi walked in just then, "Hello ladies. How are you this afternoon?" He said ladies, but the only lady he had eyes for was Memré. I glanced over at Natasha, her grin told me this should be good especially since when I looked over at Memré she was shooting daggers at him with her eyes.

"The afternoon was going great, much work happening. Why are you here? Don't you have a coffin to clean out for tonight or something?"

He smiles, "No, coffin is all clean. Would you like to

come perform a thorough…" he looks her up and down, "inspection?"

Memré blushes, which is wild because I have never seen her blush in her entire life. "No, there is nothing you possess," she glances down to his kilt-clad lap, "that I would care to inspect. Again, why are you here?"

"What a shame. I've a fine coffin that needs a thorough inspection." I am dying at this point, trying to hold in the laughter. Malachi notices and a smile ghosts across his so fast I couldn't swear it was ever there and he says, "As it happens, I was looking for the boys? Seamus, Billy, Devon, Charles? This house is monstrous big and I don't want to wander it all day trying to find someone so when I found you, I thought I would check in. Besides, it gives me a chance to nettle our Memré and she does look adorable with that blush staining her cheeks."

Memré narrows her eyes at Malachi, "I do not *blush*."

Malachi snorts, "Maybe you didn't before but you certainly did for me a moment ago, I wonder what other new things I could talk you into doing?"

"We could start with dropping you into a hole in the ground and counting the minutes while you digging yourself out."

I cut in before Malachi gets himself dropped in that hole. The twinkle in his eyes makes me think he is going to push her right to it. "Seamus has gone off with Ryna and the bodyguards on a treasure hunt assignment. Billy and Devon are somewhere in the house, I can message them for you."

Natasha cuts in, "No worries, I got Billy on his way here."

"Perfect, thanks. And Charles is off tending to his drug cartel."

Malachi murmurs, "Busy, busy. Memré, would you like to have lunch with me?"

"What?" She squawks, "No! I want to drop you twenty feet into the earth, not have lunch with you! Ugh. Go stuff yourself."

Billy walks in just in time to hear Memré, grins and says, "Come on old man, before she does something bad to you."

Twelve

PRU

I CALL Maude on the drive back to Durham. She doesn't answer but sends a text with a meeting place and time. I recognize the restaurant, she is still haunting Durham, looking for a chance to get Fate. I can't wait to talk to her. This should be quick, easy and then I can get right back to Chad. Lovely, lovely Chad.

Arriving at the restaurant I see I am not quite on time. I walk in and spot her almost immediately. She looks mad, maybe I can help her with that. Sitting down I say, "Hello Maude. How's life treating you?"

"Like utter fucking garbage because your sister is still walking the planet. I keep trying to get close to her but she has everything locked down like Fort Knox after all your stunts. Today, she sent out multiple people glamoured to look like her. I only know they were glamoured because they all left at the same time. What is she playing at?"

"Hmm, sounds like she sent her lackeys out to collect all that Charlie left behind for Amalia thinking that she would have the glamour and Fate would be dead. While he still lived. I suppose he could have predicted his own demise what with how he behaved but I don't think he wanted to look very closely at that. I came to help you. He is pointless now, just worm food."

Maude eyes me, "How exactly do you think you are going to help me? You are not a killer," she scoffs as she turns back to the food she had gotten before I arrived. "You are soft and have no control."

I snort, she isn't wrong about the person I was. But the person I was might not have killed people just to leave a house because the voice in her head told her to do it. "What I am doesn't matter. What I can provide does matter."

Maude rolls her eyes, not even bothering to hide her disdain. "And what exactly do you think you have to offer? Nail tips? Housekeeping tricks?"

"Distraction. I can get her to come out for one, and for two, I can keep her and her bodyguards occupied with me. So occupied that they forget to watch for you. I think my past history has proven that I can keep them distracted. I will need your help in finding them and knowing when she leaves the house. Tracking people is not my specialty."

The wheels are turning in Maude's head, I can almost smell the smoke. Chewing and thinking at the same time appear to be difficult for her as her jaw moves slower the deeper in thought she appears. She must not have had many very difficult targets prior to this. Or at least none that were part of the magical community and could call on shifters to aid them? Good thing my sister is just a witch and won't want to sacrifice her powers to be a vampire. Not even Charlie could talk her into giving those up, not entirely. She just hid her toys and carried on.

Maude finally swallows and looks up at me, "Ok. I see how that could be useful. I will let you know where to show up and when. Stay by your phone."

"Wonderful. Well, as stimulating as this has been, you seem to prefer your privacy. I will get out of your hair. Can't wait for your call."

Maude grunts and waves her hand in a shooing motion. My eyes narrow but luckily she isn't paying any attention to me so I turn and head for the door.

NATASHA

This foundation is a giant pain in the ass. It is coming along there are just so many little moving parts. Thank Goddess that Fate is getting me some help. The accountant will be the best thing, I hate keeping track of all this and dealing with all the financial things that will be required at some point. Admittedly, Fate has been doing more than her share since she got back from Charles place. On top of training with her parents. This life we have been dropped into is the kind of wild I never imagined possible but I am loving it. My phone starts buzzing and I see it is Grams, "Hello! How are you? I'm sorry I haven't been by lately."

"Don't worry child, I understand. You were all thrust into things much bigger than yourselves. I need to talk to you. In person. Do you mind if I pop in?"

"No, I don't mind at all. I could come see you if you want? Or pop in and we can have someone take you home if you need that later."

"No, I'll be fine. You just sit there, I'll see you in a moment."

She ends the call and I set the phone down on the table, "Grams is coming." About the time I tell Memré and Fate, my Grams pops in. She is in an open spot, with no smoke this time. And she looks… different.

Fate and Memré greet her and then excuse themselves, saying they need to go check on Trust and Kindness. Fate stops herself and thanks Grams for the tips on setting the shield for the house. Checking on Trust and Kindness is a lame excuse, but it is sweet that they would do that for me. As soon as they leave the room Grams says, "Sit child, we have many things to discuss and I put it off for much too long."

Thirteen

FATE

I HEAR everyone as they enter the house, they are jubilant with the success of the hunt, bringing in bags of stuff. I look at Devon and Charles, "Guess I need to go see what they found and hand out bonuses. Everyone on the staff gets one, even if they weren't part of the hunt."

Charles raises and eyebrow, "I am going to have to pay my guys more to keep them from asking you for a job. Calm down with the bonuses."

I laugh, "I could give your guys a bonus? Actually, I think Benny went with them to even the teams out, so whichever guys are here are getting the bonus." I shrug, "Not sorry."

He grabs me round the waist, pressing my body to his and lighting a fire I don't have time for, "We can discuss your apology later," he growls at me and then kisses me hard. He releases me and I am a little disoriented when Devon puts a hand on my neck and guides me to him. His other hand lands at the small of my back and his kisses start at the juncture of shoulder and neck causing the fire started by Charles to soar.. I let my head fall back, supported by the fingers woven into my hair. He lifts my head as he kisses along my jawline, his journey ends when he presses a soft kiss on my lips that is quickly demanding and burning hot.

He releases me, leaving his hands on me to keep me steady as I feel a little boneless. I open my eyes and realize that the fire within is also without as blue flames cover my body. "Gee, thanks guys. No one is going to guess what was happening just now…" Both of them laugh as I walk out of the billiards room, hands clenched and breathing deep to calm the flames.

By the time I make it to the living room the flames have died down but I can feel the smirks of the two men following behind me. I step into the living room and stop, jaw dropped. Devon and Charles manage to stop before they run into me though it is a close thing. There are large bags all over the place. "What is all this? Was this what you found? He had all this hidden? There must be ten bags here!"

Ryna looks back at me, "Actually, it is twenty. There are some behind the furniture as well. This man hiding these things was your husband?"

"Ugh, don't remind me. But twenty? What?"

Ajah answers this time, "Well, pretty much every place

we went had directions for the next place or set of places. We spent the day running all over the city. We were actually really glad that the vehicles all had the dark tint because damn. We had to stop and buy laundry bags to have somewhere to hide all of this, and a have better way to carry it. We did a little overkill on that but, we can just donate them somewhere."

"Any idea how much is there?"

"Well, between cash and other items, probably a few hundred million."

"What? Twenty bags wouldn't hold that much. Surely?"

Ryna opens the bag nearest her, "Some of what we found was jewels and other bank codes. There is probably a literal couple hundred million or so in cash, what did this guy do?"

"I don't actually know? I know that he bought real estate, a lot of that. But I don't know what else he did or how he got the money to start with. I can't exactly go ask… Well. Maybe I can. I should check in with my parents about that. I might be able to get some answers," I watch Ajah's eyes go wide as she realizes who else is dead that I might possibly want to talk to for answers. "I wonder if that is possible? I will share if I find any answers. For now, what if we dig out a twenty thousand dollar finders fee for everyone that works here?"

"Holy shit. I am getting Mama a house." Owen drops to a crouch, breathing heavy after his pronouncement. John and Steve draw near to him, crouching down and speaking quietly to him. I crook a finger at Brad, knowing that Ajah may be out of the loop because she has been spending a lot more time with Ryna than the guys.

Brad walks over and I ask him what is going on with Owen. He speaks so low that I wouldn't hear it if I didn't have vampire hearing, "Owen's family was kicked out of their house recently. One of the neighbors accused them of selling drugs out of the house and the owner evicted them. He has been keeping them in hotels with no idea how he was going to get them into a house because now they have an eviction on their record."

The rage I feel at hearing that, I breathe deeply to contain myself, to keep the flames that I had banked from flaring high. "Ordinarily, I would say bring them here. But that may put them in more danger than the kids should be in, let me make a quick call." I leave the room and head for the kitchen which should be far enough away for me to speak normally without everyone hearing me. I tap the screen, gently because I don't want to crack it, pull up Maggie's number and hit the call button.

She answers on the second ring, "Fate! How is the house? Are you loving it?"

"Hi Maggie, I love the house. It is exactly what we all needed. I am calling for a different issue right now. Do I have any open houses? For a family of four?"

"Hmm, let me check. I know a couple houses just opened, but they haven't been upgraded yet. I have been systematically doing the upgrades. If I know they plan to leave, I wait till they are gone. If they are staying, we do a piece at a time in the least invasive way possible. Ah, here we go. Ok, so we have a two bed and a three bed open. The three bed needs more work but would offer more space. Who is it for?"

"It's for Owen's family. They lost their place and he has been keeping them in a hotel and, well, I can't let him keep doing that. Let's put them in that three bed. Do what will keep the place decent for them as quickly as possible, they need to be in there before checkout time tomorrow. I don't want him to pay another night at some hotel. Feel free to pay the I-called-you-out-at-midnight rates for anyone willing to help with this, even if they don't ask for it. I know they won't mind having the workers in and out, inconvenient as it is. Also, tell them not to worry about the eviction. We will give them a glowing recommendation if they rent again. Charge them as little as Owen will accept. I don't need the money, and I would let them stay free while he got things sorted if he would allow it."

"You got it Fate. I just, I am so glad I met you. You are going to change the world with kindness."

"I'm trying. It is a lot easier now that I have a butt load of money. I feel like I should spread it around as much as I can."

We end the call and I make a card with Maggie's name and number on it. Walking back into the living room I head straight for Owen who is now standing and talking with everyone about his family. I interrupt, "Excuse me, sorry to interrupt. Owen, she is expecting your call. Just tell her your name."

"What did you do Ms. Owens?"

I look around expecting my adopted mother and then realize, I am Ms. Owens. Shit. "I put in a call to my real estate agent. There is a house available for your family. If I had known you needed something… I have a lot of rental properties that I inherited. Put your family in one, we have plenty and there is no reason your family should do without just because people are shitty."

I watch Owen's face get red and his eyes fill, I don't know if he is mad or sad or what. Then he takes the large step to get to me and near crushes me in a hug, fuck he is tall and really strong. He stops short of actually crushing anything in the hug, but it probably would have been a different thing if I didn't have vampire/goddess strength.

He releases me, putting those beefy hands on my shoulders, "You don't know how much this means to me. My family," he sniffs deeply to clear his snotty nose, "they are everything. Mom isn't a shifter but all her children are and Dad died a long time ago. It has been all she could do to keep the kids in line and fed. I started doing what I could almost immediately. But it has never been enough."

"Don't thank me yet, it is not in great condition. I have people going over there tonight to make sure it is livable. They are going to have to live with contractors going in and out until it is right. You can rent for as long as you want. Go on. Go call her. Get things sorted and call your mom. We will get started in here. Shoo."

He looks down at me, pats me gently on the head and sniffles his way out to the hallway. I feel eyes on me and without meeting any of them I say, "I can't help if I don't know. Tell me if you have a problem, I will help. Now let's get this done, I have other things to do tonight and I am sure you all are hungry. It smells like Maria is making enchiladas tonight."

I open the bag nearest me and start to carefully empty it while everyone else slowly moves to start with their own bag.

AJAH

Heading off to my room with Ryna after we finish dinner I look at her in the dim light. I love her more than anything. I know she wanted to take it slowly, see where things went. And we have. I know her time here is due to come to an end eventually, but I really don't want her to leave. I don't know if she wants to leave or not, but I never will if I don't just ask her. In my bedroom we strip down and crawl into bed. Snuggled up to her I bite the bullet and ask her.

"I know you wanted to see where things went between us. Well, I like where they have gone. I would like for you to stay and see how far we can take things. Because maybe this is where they are going?"

Ryna sighs and flops onto her back. "You don't know everything about me little tiger. I do bad things, admittedly, to bad people but still. You are so nice. You don't go hunting people. Feasting on their dirty blood for the joy of removing more scum from the pond."

I roll my eyes, "Listen, I don't care if you hunt down the people that spend their time hurting others. I would prefer you don't get caught. Because the paperwork for that… phew. You would probably have to fake your death to get out of prison. But, I don't mind that at all. I found a long time ago that my morals weren't as aligned with the church as most would prefer. I like an older, more feral way of dealing with things. I deal with the current laws because I have historically been pretty cash poor. The twenty thousand Fate gave me tonight? That is the largest amount of money I have ever had in my possession. Did you know that shifters are relatively long lived as that goes? We tend to live shorter lives because they are so much more violent and we are a little easier to kill than you vampire types."

"I didn't know that. My life has been somewhat insular. But, are you sure you want a vampire mate? I mean, what if we fight?"

"I'll let you kick my ass till you feel better and then kiss away your tears. But I don't think you are going to hurt me like that. And what are we going to fight about? Who does the dishes? I think we deserve to at least give us a shot. Besides, most lesbians move in after the first date, we have been seeing each other for a lot longer than a date and you still have your own bedroom. I think we will be all right."

She shifts and turns toward me. Her eyes are silvery in

the light coming from the window, "I… I have been terrified of you being taken away from me. I lived through the time when the humans would hunt you down for being with a woman, even if there was nothing, if they thought you too familiar—" she takes a breath, "I lost more than one friend that way. I still fear it. They, Seamus and Malachi, they don't know. I don't want them to know. But this is a different time. We… we can give it a try. I do love you, I just would rather walk away than see you die."

I pull her closer, "I will try really hard to avoid that."

"I would very much appreciate that."

Fourteen

FATE

IT IS TRAINING day once again, I am eager to see my parents. Even if it does mean another grueling training session. My powers have grown exponentially. I know they will be pleased as the general idea is that I need to become a fully realized goddess as soon as possible to have the safety of godhood from Demeter and the Beast.

The guys both slept in my bed last night, I had cuddles from both sides and I love it. I could deal with that being a nightly occurrence, I just don't know how to work out the sex in a way that will make everyone happy. Guess I will figure it out eventually. For now, I am the last one still upstairs and I need to eat before we leave.

I make it downstairs and Maria has breakfast burritos and coffee waiting for me. She seems more at ease than I have ever seen her and I am glad for it. I scarf the food as quickly as possible and suck down the coffee like it is life. I quickly put my dishes in the dishwasher and head for the billiard room where I am pretty sure the boys are waiting for me. They are both staring at the pool table and don't notice when I enter the room so I walk up behind the two of them and quickly grab the backs of their shirts, porting us to the Underworld before they can turn around and see who it is that has grabbed them.

As soon as our feet rest on the ground outside my parents home I let go and leap back before the boys can retaliate. Charles laughs and Devon kicks back in a spin that brings him to face in my direction before he realizes that Charles is laughing and we are in the Underworld so it could have only been me that grabbed them.

Devon grins at me and launches himself at me, landing lightly in front of me and still tackling me to the ground his face buried in my neck as he bites it lightly over and over which tickles like mad. Eventually we realize that Cerberus is standing over us and Devon releases me, as soon as Cerberus smiles I know. I roll myself at his feet and he does a little hop with his front paws, landing and leaning down to lick a long stripe up Devon's back just as he starts to roll away. Charles grabs my feet and snatches me out from under Cerberus. Unfortunately Devon gets part of that lick to his face, and the resultant yelling and cursing seems to make Cerberus chuckle as he trots over to us. I pet him while Charles quickly steps behind me and back a couple steps. I am entertained and tell Cerberus, "Come on, cutie. Let's go find mom and dad, leave these two to sort themselves out."

I create a towel and toss it back to Devon, he grins at me as he catches it. The two of them follow along behind us as we enter the house. We find Hades and Persephone in the training room waiting for us. Hades see Devon carrying the towel and still looking a little sticky, "I see we need to start working on reaction time. My daughter looks incredibly dry considering as she is the one I sent Cerberus after."

"Dad!"

"What? You should be faster than they are and obviously you were. Cerberus? Care to explain?"

My father laughs out loud at the explanation, "Oh yes, Devon, reaction time training. You should have been moving the minute you felt the change in her. She rolled at Cerberus not knowing I had sent him for her, but had it been a different creature, she would have been in the path of harm. And you would have been no help. Let's go boys. Cerberus, go fetch your mates. We are playing a new game today."

I watch Cerberus blink out as the boys follow behind Hades. Poor guys. Then I look to my mother, Persephone. She no longer wears the guise her mother Demeter insists upon when she is there. She is dark and glorious now, her skin is brown but with this blue glow to it that makes her stunning. Her hair is long and blue-black but today it is tamed into a braid. Instead of the flowing dress she came home in, today she is all leather and lace. I feel underdressed in my lycra, but I know she isn't at all concerned with what I wear.

"Hi Mom, so what are we doing today?"

"Today we test your strength, see how far you have come since last we saw you. And before you leave I will teach you the safe charms, we use them mostly for the pups, but you may want to put them to use on anyone that isn't difficult to kill. Or well, anyone that isn't a god, because at some point Demeter will attack you."

She turns and walks off toward a partitioned area and I follow. Coming around the partition I see what look like ballistics dummies lined up against the far wall. She stops and turns to me, "First, we are going to blow up the dummies. Watch as I do this one and then see if you can repeat it."

I watch as she flings her arm toward the dummies and the power flies out in a straight line, hitting the middle dummy and blowing him into a thousand tiny bits. She looks over at me and I nod. Nerves in my throat going wild I swing my arm out in an arc, aiming to release and hit the dummy to the right of the one she hit. I release a little early though and hit one two spaces to the left of the one she hit. It does explode though, so partial success, but my aim is shit.

Persephone asks, "Was that the one you meant to hit?"

"No, I was aiming for the one directly to the right of the one you hit."

"Still, not bad daughter mine," nodding in approval, "aim takes practice and we can put those dummies back over and over till you start hitting what you aim at and you did hit one of them on the first try rather than the wall or falling short."

I practice blowing up dummies until my arms are ready to fall off. Then Mom runs her hands over my arms, I feel a cool energy go through them and they feel great, like when we started.

Stepping back she says, "We are done practicing that for today. Now we see how much of my abilities you inherited. I know you got your father's flames and some of his other abilities I can see in you. This one, well, it is much like what he can do only… not. Watch carefully."

She waves a hand at the dummies on the far wall and I see a line of shadows slip into the dummies, one shadow for each dummy. She waits till everyone is settled in and then calls a dummy to her, it flies across the room, the neck smacking into her hand opened and waiting to grip a throat. As soon as it lands, before the legs swing forward with the momentum her other hand darts forward into the dummy without creating a hole and closes on the shadow within, snatching it out of the dummy. She holds the shadow up for me to see, the dummy is the same as it was before she called it over. The soul is also intact, but all the threads that bound it to the dummy are broken. Ragged looking ends, and the ripping sound as she pulled the soul out, I don't think it was an actual sound that anyone could hear.

"Mom, that was wild. Does Dad know you can do this? Does Demeter know?"

She stuffs the shadow back in the dummy, holding it there and sending some energy through it to reattach the ragged ends. "Yes, your father knows. Demeter does not. Most don't know because I kept it quiet, never using it in front of anyone until after I married your father. So the few that do know think that your father gifted me that ability when I became queen here. I prefer they think that, it keeps them from knowing the kind of power I hold in my own right. It is most always going to be better if your enemy underestimates you. Avoid showing your full power. Before you leave here today, you will activate your flames and then glamour yourself so that no one sees them outside your family. We don't want everyone to know how much you took after either of us. Now, see if you can do what I just did."

I hold my hand out and call the dummy to me as she sends hers back across the room. When is hits my hand I focus on reaching the shadow within and my hand slips into the body like it doesn't exist, only the shadow is real. My hand closes around it and I yank it out, the ripping not really a sound is awful. I look to my mom and she has clapped her hands together, holding them in prayer fashion in front of her lips, tears leaking down her face.

"You are so amazing and I am so very proud of you. You are near fully activated, I think this is the quickest it has ever happened. Though I can't think of another time in which it would have needed to happen so quickly. Ok, now put the shadow back and heal the threads, then send it back to the wall with the others."

I do as she says asking, "Does that ripping ever get better and can everyone hear it?"

"No. The only one that has ever heard it or can even see that you are holding a soul is your father or Hecate, oh, I forgot. She knows too. But she knows a lot of things that no one told her. She doesn't hear the sound but she knows about it and can see the souls."

"So that is just something we hear, I wonder why?"

"Hecate may have it blocked. But it isn't completely a sound, it doesn't make waves the way sounds do. Which may be why only certain ones can hear it, those that are attuned to the world of souls. Now practice it some more. Till you don't have to think about it."

We practice that until we hear my father Hades walking back with the guys. I send the most recent dummy back as Persephone says, "All right, let's see those flames."

I close my eyes for a second and focus, I feel the flames spring up all over. Opening my eyes I see mom Smiling at me, head tipped to one side. She says, "I just love getting to work with you and see you do these things so quickly. You are amazing. Now glamour."

She looks so serious so quickly, I pop the glamour up without even thinking about it. She claps and throws her arms around me. "Yes! Perfect!" Dad, Devon, and Charles round the corner just as my mom releases me.

Dad smiles and walks a little faster to come hug the both of us. I feel so loved, tears slip down my face because I have never felt loved like this by my adopted parents and it is just so much good. My heart feels like it is spilling over with joy. Dad releases us and asks, "How did the training go?"

"She is nearly there! Our girl will be fully activated within the next couple days. Fate, take down the glamour so your father can get a look at you."

I do as she says and his smile gets so big. Mom hugs him with one arm and his goes round her. I can feel their approval like sunlight on my soul. The guys step up next to me, one on either side and each slips an arm around me.

Hades nods in approval, "Your flames recognize them as not a danger to you. Very good. You should know, if someone that is a danger to you touches you they will burn. It is less effective on certain Gods and Goddesses, but it is another weapon. Oh, and it is particularly effective on earth types. Like Demeter." He says the last with a wicked grin and my mother hugs him tight with her own answering grin. They are adorable. I love them so much.

They give me directions on keeping on with using my abilities and how to recognize when I am fully activated. The guys listen in very intently to that last part, as they know how important it is for me to be fully activated before Demeter finds us. Mom pulls me off to the side just before we leave; she shows me how to create the safe charms and hugs me one more time before shooing me off.

MEMRÉ

I have been holed up in my suite away from everyone today. Natasha is working with Billy, the bodyguards are training with Ryna and Seamus, and Fate has taken Devon and Charles with her to train. Maybe I should start my own training regimen, or maybe I should see what Maria has going in the kitchen instead. An argument could be made, and has been by Fate and Natasha, that I have been hiding all these years because I didn't want to deal with my scars from the last idiot I married and had a child with. They are wrong though. I dealt with that. Realized it wasn't my fault that he stayed undetected for so long, that is what people who are doing wrong do. They hide shit. From everyone. I am going for food, thinking about it I haven't had anything to eat since roughly yesterday.

On my way to the kitchen I smell a ghost of Malachi's cologne. A piercing need runs through me and I stuff it back down where it belongs. He may be sexy as sin and a kilt-wearing work of ivory art, but he is also annoying, overbearing, pig-headed, and just plain not right for me at all. My lady parts be damned. They don't know what they are talking about and all that quivering is easily taken care of with one of my toys.

I make it to the kitchen with no run-ins. He must have gone to join in with the training. Maria is amazing, she sees me and tells me to sit, within minutes she has this loaded omelet in front of me along with this fragrant hot tea. "What kind of tea is this? It smells so nice and tastes even better."

"Hibiscus rose. It helps with grounding and is good for the heart." She looks over st me, "I think you need the help with the heart. You are too closed off. Life goes on and hiding doesn't make it stop."

My eyes popped open, holy crap. This woman just handed me the best omelet I have ever had with a side of get your shit together. I mumble, "I'll keep that in mind," and tuck into my omelet so I can get myself out of the kitchen. Within minutes I shovel the omelet I wanted to savor into me and suck down the tea. Careful to put my dishes in the dishwasher, I make it out of the kitchen without any further pearls of wisdom about my heart.

Of course she isn't wrong, but the only guy floating around here that has shown the least bit of interest— oof! Lost in thought I have run into a wall of, I step back and look up, ah hell. Malachi. Of course it would be Malachi. Why are his pupils so big? I glance down and realize I put my hands up when I ran into him and they are still resting on his very firm pectorals. Oh my. Hands down! Not that down! Off the vampire dammit!

I take another step back, why am I so hot suddenly? "Sorry about that. I was lost in thought."

He smirks at me, "I see that," he takes a step closing the gap my two steps had opened between us, "but I rather liked your hands on me and the feeling of you pressed against me was very nice too." His voice is low and I have to focus to hear all of what he is saying. "You could feel free to pretend to push me away now if that would help you feel like you fought the attraction you have for me."

My eyes fly open to see those incredibly firm pecs staring me in the eye so to speak and I do exactly what he said, putting my hands right back on him and push. He moves less than an inch back and the bastard grins. I want to yell at him but a lot of me is on fire right now and I can't seem to find any oxygen in this room. It is filled with him, just like I want to be.

His arms come round me, one on my waist and the other weaves fingers into my hair. No one has touched my hair in so long, when his fingers curl and tug lightly my eyelids flutter closed and my head drops back to follow the pleasure of it. "I wasn't going to until you came to me but, how can I resist when you melt for my touch?" I feel his lips touch mine and the world explodes in fire. My fingers clutch at his chest as I deepen the kiss, pressing upward by raising up on my toes. His hand tightens in my hair and my tongue slips in his mouth eliciting a moan from him. Then he wrests control back from me, his arms pressing me closer as he deepens the kiss while lifting me off my feet.

He groans and breaks the kiss, for long moments the only sound is that of our heavy breathing. He lets me slide down his body till my feet touch the floor again and I can feel the push of him through his kilt because he does not wear a sporran. Releasing my hair and moving both of his hands to my shoulders he says, "Memré, if you don't want to take this any farther right now you should run away. Or we are going to find the nearest room with a door and talk about the things between us." He drags a rough breath in and steps back from me.

I touch my lips with hands that miss his chest and I hear voices down the hall. My eyes widen, not ready for everyone to know about this! Not ready for that conversation with Natasha. I clear my throat, "Excuse me, I need to go… tend my files." I rush out of there to the sound of his rich laughter and I think seriously about going back but instead I make a beeline for my nice quiet suite where things like this don't happen.

Fifteen

FATE

WAKING up the morning after a hard training day to no muscle pain is the best thing about all this change I have been dumped into since Charlie died. I thought that day was the end of my life and now I have eternity stretching out before me. Devon stayed with me last night, he is working hard to make sure he stays better than Charles still. If he ever asks me I could tell him that they are equally talented in different ways. Sex with one is nothing like sex with the other. With Devon it is passion and love and need. Charles is fire and thunder and rough in the best way. I love them both for the men they are, even the parts that aren't so shiny. Both of them have gone downstairs already, we had our morning coffee in bed. I haven't had to get my own coffee once since I added Charles to this mix, I have to say it is a great bonus.

But now, now I need to get moving. I had my shower already and came back to lay in the bed for a little while. I thought being a goddess would be a little less work? It would seem not. Today we all need to go visit Devon's place and check for anything left behind while Natasha and I get the interior dimensions of the house back to what they were before we arrived.

Thirty minutes later everyone has gathered up and Griselda is here with us. I don't know why she showed up but I am really happy she did. I love seeing her, she is like the grandmother I will never have. Logistics figured out we all load up and start our caravan to the other place.

Devon's house looks a little forlorn, sitting empty. He is going to have to rent it to a nice family so it won't be lonely. We all pile out and go wandering through the place. Natasha, Griselda, and myself all walk through rooms releasing spells that altered space and fixing any dings or paint scrapes that happened during the move.

Everyone else goes through the rooms ahead of us to look for forgotten things, or things intentionally left behind for collecting at a later date. Like the extra spell books, we wanted them safe until we were relatively sure there would be no fuckery about in regards to the ghost. But she has so far, been mostly very shy and hasn't bothered anyone. If she watches people showering, well, she isn't letting them know or bothering anyone with it so whatever. I walk down the stairs after fixing the room that was my office, Devon and Charles carried down the books left tucked away in there. I make it outside just in time to see my sister pull up. Wonderful. I hurry outside to intercept her and see Charles makes it to her before I do, love that man.

I can see her talking quietly to him and I move to stand near Devon, all of the body guards are milling about the yard in seemingly random spaces but they all look pretty well spaced out to make a direct charge at me nearly impossible. I hear Griselda behind me, "She isn't what you need to focus on."

Without taking my eyes off Pru I ask, "What do you mean?"

"She is the distraction, not the threat."

My eyes widen as what she said hits me, "Where is the threat Griselda?" Devon is scanning the area now as am I.

"I don't know, I am old and my eyes are older. But Pru is not the threat right now."

I see a flash and feel the bullet tear through my right shoulder. I hear Griselda cry out behind me and Natasha's screams. Before I think about what I am doing I put my hand out and call the person that shot me to my left hand. Her throat hits my hand and I grip her tightly as I recognize her, good old Maude the shitty housekeeper. I reach into her chest and grab her soul, snatching it from her body and throwing the body back and away from me. I hold the soul up before me, "My parents will hold you till I can come take care of you myself." I send her directly to my mother knowing that she will feel my magic on Maude and begin to question her, I think she may be the more vicious of the two. If she torments Maude till I get there, well, who am I to gainsay the Queen of the Underworld?

I hear Natasha sobbing, and I turn around to see Griselda on the ground. She has lost a good deal of blood and what is left is flowing slow. Her breathing is shallow as I hear Pru's car pealing around a corner. I don't care about Pru, she is nothing to me. But the two women in front of me are family in a way that she never was or will be. I hear Natasha saying, "Why didn't you tell me it would be today?"

Griselda smiles a weak smile, "Child, I didn't know what day it would be only that it would be. I thought I would die in my sleep or something. I am glad I could be here with you all though. You need to know, Pru will not stop and neither will that other that is after you. They are grown desperate because the one you call the beast is nearing the end of his power to withstand the curse upon him. He needs the body you would provide him. He—" she coughs a bit, her face twisted in pain, "I love you both more than you know. Natasha, you remember what I told you. We are the guardians and you must take up the mantle."

The ambulance arrives and I realize we have a second dead body and one gunshot. I turn to look at Maude's body but it is gone. Charles pats my shoulder, saying in a whisper, "No worries love, some of us have been criminals for a long time. She is back where she had been hiding."

I mouth thank you to him as the paramedics do their best to save Griselda. She sits up and steps away from her body, Natasha doesn't see her leave. Griselda looks up and sees me watching her.

"Fate, you will watch over her?" I nod so as not to alert anyone else that I can see Griselda is already gone from her body. "Good. Make sure she remembers to get the note from my nightstand drawer and that she must say the words. Want me to pass anything on to your parents?"

I whisper and encase it in the wind so only Griselda can hear it, "Tell them I want to speak to Maude when I come next and that I would like to bring Natasha to visit you sometimes. I think it would help her."

Griselda smiles a watery kind of smile, "You were always too good for those idiots that adopted you. I am so glad that you have your parents now. I am also glad that Natasha has her Billy," she nods over to where he is holding her and rubbing small circles on her back, "he isn't making her grief less, just holding her while she processes it. I feel that is the best we can hope for sometimes, a person to hold us while we grieve. I must go, I feel the pull of the Underworld. I love you all."

She fades away and I know she is with my parents now, relaying all that has just come to pass. The paramedics have called it, and they covered Griselda's body with a sheet.

The officers that arrived at the same time have been speaking with our bodyguards, Ajah comes to me and says, "They want to speak to you."

I remember I was shot and it is likely that the paramedics will want to see it as soon as they realize that. The wound is healed already but I place a seeming of the injury in that spot. It isn't the most pleasant thing, but it will keep it appearing as an injury until the EMTs can tend it. I walk over to the officers with Devon and Charles trailing behind me.

"Ma'am, I'm sorry to bother you but—" he looks up and notices my shoulder, "Holy shit, do you know you were shot? Medic! We need someone over here!"

One of the EMTs walks over, looks at my shoulder and says, "I need you to come over here with me, so I can get a proper look at that."

I nod and walk over to the ambulance, taking a deep breath as I do, and I smell wolf. I slant my eyes over at him and he grins a wolfish sort of grin.

I sit on the bumper of the ambulance and he looks around. Seeing no humans anywhere near us he says quietly, "I am exactly what you think I am though I cannot place exactly what you are. You smell like witch and vampire and something… I can't place the last one but good Goddess it smells good." He shakes his head, "I can also smell that while you were shot, you are not bleeding. I would guess you are healed already. If I move the cloth what will anyone glancing in this direction see?"

"They will see you checking out the injury on my shoulder. I made it appear to be there, it isn't the most comfortable thing ever but it means that you can inspect it with no worries."

He snips the neckline of my shirt enough to be able to get a good view of the wound, "May I touch it? This looks really incredibly life-like."

"Yes, just don't go trying to dig any bullets out, there is

a matching hole on the back of my shoulder from where it passed through me and hit Griselda."

"No worries, the wound is not the hole I want to play with on you." He grins at my shocked face and I laugh. He cleans up the area where the wound appears to be and slaps some bandages on it. "Guessing the two hulks staring daggers at my back belong to you?"

I look over to see Charles and Devon both staring hard, "Hmm," I smile, "yes, they are mine. I don't think they like you very much."

He grins, unrepentant, "That's ok. I am more concerned with whether or not you like me and I don't mind waiting in line. Especially," he inhales deeply, "if you walk around smelling like this. How are they not walking around hard all the time?"

I blush and then Charles is next to me, sticking his hand out to the EMT, "Hello, I'm Charles and you are?"

The grinning wolf EMT takes his hand and says, "Hi Charles, I'm Julian. I have to finish making it look like I have tended her wound or the cops aren't going to believe it."

"Well, get on with it Juli, we do have other things to do and eventually they are going to find the body of the shooter. Who, by the way, happened to shoot herself. Isn't that lucky Fate?"

I bite back a grin, "Yes it is. That will make it much easier for the officers to wrap this investigation up."

"Your name is Fate? Hmm, sounds meant to be." I blush again and Charles growls, Julian chuckles, "No worries Char, lady Fate is safe with me." He pulls out a clip board, "We just need to take down some information and I will release you as not an emergency and that you plan to follow up with your own doctor."

I fill out the information and hand the clipboard back to him. He looks it over and then grabs a small notebook, writes something on it and hands it back to me with a grin, "Looks like you missed one thing."

I smile at him as I read 'Fate's phone number' across the top of the notepad and I say "Cheeky wolf!" Charles narrows his eyes at me as I write on the notepad. I just smile wider as Julian rocks on his heels with a grin firmly in place.

I hand the clipboard back and Julian steps back, "The officials await m'lady."

I laugh as I walk away and Charles says, "What was that about?"

I shrug, "He asked for my number."

"Did you give it to him?"

About that time Devon's phone starts ringing. He looks at the screen, looks past us and I hear Julian start laughing. Charles catches up as I grin and Devon gets on the same page when Charles starts to laugh. "I see Juli isn't the only cheeky thing around here today."

We have Griselda's body picked up by a local witch funeral home. They promise to dress her and keep her body preserved until we are ready to dispose of it. Just in case they get ideas I let them know I have a direct line to the Underworld, this body is not the one to tamper with and the soul especially needs to remain untouched as it is with my parents right now. One of them got snotty and asked who my parents are anyway. She paled when I told her.

The officers find the body while I am dealing with the morticians and we are called over to see if we recognize her. Devon says, "Yes, that is my former housekeeper. She was really nasty to Fate here when we first started dating and I had to let her go. I guess she really held a grudge against Fate for that. I don't think Fate knew her from anywhere else, did you Fate?"

I tell them, "I met her twice here in this house. She was awful and he fired her. I never saw her again till now."

We wrap things up with the officers who are pretty certain it will be ruled as a murder/suicide, since Maude killed Griselda and then appeared to have shot herself with a handgun. They say they will call if they need anything else and we thank them before getting ourselves back across the street. It feels like Natasha is hanging on by a thread and she needs to get home. The ambulance has left and the funeral home van has left with Griselda. The officers are still parked in the street maintaining a perimeter but we have leave to go. Devon locks up the house and we all load up for the drive home.

Sixteen

PRU

DEMETER HAS MOVED herself closer to Durham but still says she needs to remain outside the city for various reasons. After the shooting goes so badly I screech my way out of there. I hate how disappointed Charles looked, but there is nothing for it. I make it to the address she gave me about an hour and a half after I leave. She comes to the door to welcome me when I arrive asking, "Did you get her? Is it done?"

I wring my hands as I tell her the story of how I got Maude to help me and I distracted Fate and everyone else just like we planned but Maude's aim was off and she hit Fate in the right shoulder, the bullet passed through clean and Fate used her air magic to snatch Maude out of her hiding place.

Demeter grows angrier with every word I say till

finally she yells, "Silence! You failed me. You are sure that she only used air to drag Maude out? Nothing else?"

"Yes," I answer keeping my eyes pointed to the ground, "I felt the winds pass me to go after Maude. Fate has used them around me so often that I would recognize that feeling anywhere."

"Well then, all is not lost and she is probably weakened now. Have some food and when my lover arrives we will discuss what to do next."

"Yes Demeter." I walk over to the table laden with various foodstuffs, I am not actually hungry but it won't do to offend Demeter by not eating her food. I am learning that she does not appreciate being denied and I have a feeling that the consequences could be bad. I would ask what I got myself into again except, I don't think I did. I think I was signed up for this by my parents. Much the same way they signed me up to be Fate's babysitter. I wasn't asked but what was I going to do? Tell them no? That wouldn't have been okay and plus, Fate was always plotting how to not be noticed. And trying to stop me from seeing what she had going on in there, why would she unless she had things to hide?

The food is well cooked. I was hungry. I think I need to feed again soon, but I can do that while I am out next. The food has a strange aftertaste to it. I don't know what it is, it isn't a poison, and I don't know that a poison would do any good on me. But there is something about this food…

Demeter watches me eat, chatting about how nice it is to be out in the world again. She tells me she was falsely imprisoned for a long time, all because she tried to take what was rightfully hers to begin with, as one owns one's children. You carry them in your body, give them the gift of life, they belong to you for so long as you live. That is just how it should be, even though not everyone agrees with that particular theory.

I look at her in surprise, "You know, you're right. If you have a child they belong to you. As do their progeny, because they wouldn't be there if not for you. My parents certainly owned me while they were living and they made sure I did their bidding. Fate rebelled, she wouldn't do as they said even though she would have been stuck in some orphanage for her whole life if they hadn't picked her up. But was she grateful? No! Not once in all her life was she grateful or anything other than a burden to me and my parents!"

Demeter smiles, "Just so dear, just so. She really must pay for all her crimes. And we will make sure she does, you and I. And my dear beast. He is so much better at these things than I am, he will be here very soon, but he prefers to travel by more conventional methods."

"Good. She has a lot of protection now, I think we do need help. Where is he coming from?"

"Oh, don't you worry about that. He will be here in a couple days. It was quite far away, a little place no one has heard of anymore."

"Now that I have eaten, I am really quite sleepy. Would you mind if I laid down some where?"

"Not at all, you go sleep in that first bedroom. Sleep till I tell you to wake."

Something strange about the way she said that, but my brain is too fuzzy. I need to lay down, I am so very sleepy all of a sudden.

Seventeen

FATE

TODAY IS the day for Griselda's funeral. We are doing it at home, well, her home. She told Natasha that she wanted to be cremated, so her body couldn't be raised or cut up or used for nefarious purposes once she was gone. We have decided to build the pyre in her back yard and I will funnel the smoke so it is not noticeable, I figured out a filtration system that should do the trick.

Memré and I are going to cast the spell to keep Griselda's home unseen until Natasha chooses otherwise. The place doesn't exist on the tax rolls, so no worries there. But first, we have to get there. The funeral home witches agreed to arrive at one, so we have plenty of time and thank goodness for that. Natasha has been holed up in her room since we got back. I have been in to see her and so has Memré, but she is sad and staying holed up for now. I feel like she will get better in her own time and I can't rush her. Even today, if she takes her sweet time, we will just sit and wait for her.

I don't think she will though, her Grams was too important to her. She might be broken for a while but I think today she will pretend, for her Gram's wishes and for her mother. Her mother and father will be there today though they aren't overly much into the magical community, they are not unaware of it. From what I understand roughly half the magical community of Durham will be in attendance as well. Maybe I should order food? Wait. We are in the south. There will be food and more brought. What I should do is send someone for alcohol. Grams would love that but I don't know that she has enough in her house to provide for that many at once.

I head downstairs, I only just finished getting dressed and the guys are in their rooms getting ready now. I see Owen coming out of the billiards room and I call out to him. He ambles over, "What ya need Miss Fate?"

"I need someone to go on a booze run. Griselda was well loved in the magical community and many of them will want to celebrate her life though we will miss her. So I need you to go buy a ridiculous amount of booze. Take two vehicles and make sure to get mixers and ice. Oh, and garbage bags and disposable stuff for eating. Everyone is going to bring food, we need lots."

He looks a little concerned, "How many people do you think will be there?"

"Probably a few hundred. They won't likely all come

at once, but the word is out that she passed and they will be coming to pay their respects. I am going to get the guys to organize the security, because we don't want everyone wandering all over her house and some will come in search of opportunity."

Owen brings his hands together and cracks his knuckles loudly, "That would not be okay. I would not like it if anyone tried to steal from that nice old woman, even if she is dead now. And that would really hurt Natasha's feelings more too. That would not do. I'll be on the security detail too, won't I?"

I put a hand on his arm, "Of course you will." I call some money from my purse into my hand, "Here you go. Take this and at least one other someone and try to buy out a liquor store."

He salutes, "Yes ma'am!" He leaves with a grin, shouting for Steve.

I continue on my way to the kitchen. Maria comes over and hugs me, "I knew her before I came her, she was a good lady and I will miss her."

As she releases me I say, "Me too. Are you coming to the funeral?"

"Only if you let me organize the food line. I hate being idle at a funeral, too much time for crying. If I am doing something I can comfort people and feel useful."

"That would be wonderful. I know Natasha will appreciate that. She is grieving hard, Griselda was her favorite person."

"I can see why. Here, let me get you the coffee. Do you

want a bite? I know there will be food all day but I have things if you are hungry now?"

"No, just the coffee please. I am not ready to eat yet. Oh, no worries about utensils, the boys are picking up disposable things and lots of garbage bags."

"Good, good. Here is the coffee. Sit while you drink, it will go down better."

I chuckle and have a seat. Maria isn't normally this concerned but I think it is how she deals with her sadness. Personally I tuck it away to take out and look at when I am alone and can grieve without anyone seeing me cry because I don't share those emotions with anyone if I can help it. Not the healthiest thing but oh well. It is where I am at for now.

Devon and Charles walk into the kitchen looking very nice in their matching suits. They walk over and one on each side kiss my cheek. Maria bustles over with coffee and makes them sit as well. They laugh good naturally and yes ma'am her as they sit down. I talk to them about the plans for the day, letting them know about Owen and Steve making the liquor run, how Maria will be organizing the food, and that I want them to head up the security. Billy has his job with tending Natasha, and that is as it should be. But with a few hundred people wandering about in Griselda's house, we need people to mind things and watch over everyone.

"Because above all, we are not going to let some jackass steal from Griselda while we lay her to rest and make Natasha even more sad than she already is. Natasha said last night that Griselda laid a spell on the house that no one can go in it until Natasha goes there and lets the spell down, it was set to be activated on her death."

Charles nods, "Good thinking on her part. How many times have people tried to breach it already?"

"Last night when I talked to her Natasha said there had already been five separate attempts."

Devon shakes his head, "That is terrible. Why would anyone try to break into her house as soon as she dies?"

"For the books and the trinkets. Natasha and I talked about it last night, we are going to send all the books here after we get there, I will pop them into her room. And she we will go through the house quickly to find any trinkets that shouldn't necessarily be in the hands of people that would steal them. Those are getting popped into her room as well. After that I will lay a layer of air over everything upstairs because nobody should be upstairs messing with anything. She isn't sure about her mom, so if she shows up before we finish, I want you two to stall her and the husband. Okay?"

They nod, and Devon says, "Sounds like a good plan. Are we ready to head over?"

I see Natasha enter the kitchen, looking stunning in her black dress and matching pumps. She left her hair down today and it is like a short cape of spun silk hanging behind her. "Yes, we are ready to go. I take it you have let them know about security detail?"

"I did. And I got the boys to go get a mountain of booze along with a few other things. Maria offered to head up the food table. So we have everything covered. After the first part, you will be in the clear and can grieve as you need, we will ensure that everyone behaves."

An hour later we are all over at Griselda's house. I place a second barrier over the one that Griselda set, just in case anyone is waiting around back for it to drop. Natasha nods her thanks and I touch her shoulder briefly. Squaring her shoulders and taking a deep breath she touches the barrier that Griselda set and it drops in a shower of sparkles that swirl around Natasha before dissolving into nothing. She turns, "It feels like she hugged me." Tears run unchecked down her face and for once, mine.

I feel two idiots out back bounce off the barrier I put in place so I say, "Come, let's get inside. We should hurry before anyone shows up again."

She nods and we all head up the driveway, I look back and shield our vehicles too, I am in no mood for fuckery today. Walking into Griselda's house without her presence to warm it is hard. I can only imagine it is even more diffi-cult for Natasha. She is holding herself together though, the only sign is the tears running down her face. I call a package of tissues to me and pass them to her.

"Thanks. Let's get those books. She kept them in the basement."

She and Billy head down, I pause at the top of the stairs to tell Devon and Charles, "There are two out back looking for a way in. Expect more. Don't worry about the vehicles, I shielded them too."

They nod and go talk to our bodyguards, we brought some of Charles's other guys with us today too. As I turn to follow them downstairs Charles asks, "Can we all move freely through the barrier you put up?"

"Yes, why?"

"Thought we could have some fun before you all come back up."

"Go ahead. Make sure you know who or what you are dealing with, no one gets injured today of all days. Keep and eye out for the mortuary witches too."

I make it down the stairs and Natasha is directing Billy as he stacks the books carefully after placing each in a cloth sack meant to protect them from dust or sunlight or bugs outside this basement which has been heavily spelled to keep everything from decaying. I stand next to Natasha and bump her shoulder lightly with mine. She bumps me back and I know she will be all right. Today will suck but she will get through. Billy gets all the books stacked and Natasha looks to me, "Are you sure you can move all this? There must be two hundred books stacked there."

"I can, and no problem. Being a goddess has its perks and this is one of them." I close my eyes and picture the layout of Natasha's room, we cleared a space for these last night. I picture the stacks of books there in the space and I feel the power move through me as the books go where they are meant to be. Then I feel the process my parents warned me about and I shout, "Oh hell, it's about to get really bright in here! Run and close the door behind you!"

My body has already started to glow and is getting brighter by the second as Billy and Natasha put on the speed to get out of the basement before I go supernova bright. I am so grateful to be in a basement for this, as I drop to my knees with the power coursing through my body. A breeze kicks up around me and I close my eyes to shut out the brightness emanating from me. The breeze rockets to a hurricane around me and then dies down just as fast before fading away completely. I chance cracking open an eyelid to see if I am done going supernova and it is dark again in the basement. Mostly. My flames are on again and the lights that were on down here have all popped. I point at the bulbs and fix them one at a time. My parents told me I should do a few small magics after this to ground myself and establish a base so that I wouldn't do a big thing by accident. And I see why when a little too much juice hits one bulb and it explodes entirely.

I hear the door to the basement creak open just a bit and then Devon says, "You good now? We covered the edges with our jackets but if there are any windows down there it is guaranteed someone saw that."

"I'm fine," I say as I head for the stairs, "great actually. I am also a fully activated goddess. I guess moving the books tipped me right over the edge."

I make it up the stairs to find Devon and Charles hovering, they both give me a thorough look over to be sure I am not lying about being ok. I chuckle and turn a circle for them, "Satisfied now? I really am ok. Where is Natasha?"

Devon answers saying, "She grabbed a basket and started collecting trinkets. She said Griselda didn't keep any in the basement so there was no reason for her not to get this done while you finished what you were doing. She had the utmost faith that you would be fine."

"Well, she knows I would never leave her when she needs me. Did Memré say when she would be here?"

Ajah answers, "She said two-ish, she doesn't want to see them move Griselda's body into place."

"Ah. I understand. Thank you." I head upstairs to find Natasha and Billy. I guess find isn't quite the right word as I could feel where they were. I find them in one of the spare bedrooms, little trinkets all over it. The basket Billy carries is huge and nearly over flowing. I loop a barrier of air around it so nothing will fall out but Natasha can keep dropping things in.

She drops the last item in the room into the basket, "I have been putting off going into her room. I don't think I can do it."

I walk over and hug her, "Do you want me to do it for you?"

"I, yes please. I was hoping you would offer."

"Anything for you. You just sit down, Billy will wait with you. I will call in another basket."

Billy sets his basket down and I go ahead and port that thing into their room at the house. Calling in another basket I hook it over my arm and head for Griselda's room.

I don't want to go in either but, I am better able to handle it right now than she is. Opening the door I reach over and flip the light switch. It looks like she never left. And I guess, why wouldn't it? I miss her already. I walk around the room and collect anything that feels like it even has residual magic. Letters? Into the basket. Note for Natasha in the nightstand? Into the basket. Diary? Basket. Looking over Griselda's jewelry I realize the majority of it is trinkets that hold some sort of magic. I poof the lot over to Natasha's room, and then I create a duplicate of all of it, sans power. The box and everything that was in it appear to still be sitting there. If Natasha decides to give her mother some of it that is her choice. But she will not worry about it today. I check the drawers and the closet, finding a couple of secret compartments. Everything goes in the basket. After I finish I stand in the middle of the room and casting out my power I ask that anything that should go but hasn't been found to set itself in my hand. Four different charms land gently in my hand. I sweep the room with my power once more, just in case and nothing else comes out. The room feels as empty as it is. "Good-bye Griselda."

I leave the empty room and I cast the spell that puts a layer over everything to keep what shouldn't be taken from being removed from the house. I step into the spare bedroom where Natasha waits with her Billy, "It is done. I sent your Gram's jewelry over, box and all. Most of it was magic. I also duplicated everything and put it right back so if your mom is looking for a piece, she can have it and unless she is looking for the magic, she will never notice. And this basket," I hold out the large basket in front of me, "is near as full as the other." I send that to Natasha's room as well. "The house is set now, no one will be able to steal furniture or anything. And we will all know if they try because their fingers will be stained bright, bright pink. With the exception of the jewelry box, because it is a fake so they can have it."

Natasha lets a small giggle escape, "Thank you. I don't know what I would do without all of you. You and Billy especially. Do we need to worry about anyone going to the house?"

I laugh, "No, I don't think we do. Malachi is there, as is Seamus. Trust and Kindness are prowling the estate, ever hopeful someone will fuck up. Plus, it is shielded pretty well regularly. Woe betide any fool that tries to run in as Memré heads this way. She is in a foul mood right now and she might just wrap them in rocks and leave them as chew toys for the puppies, she does love those puppies. I think she would find it really entertaining."

Natasha sniffles a little, wipes her eyes and stands. "It should be about time for the death witches to arrive, I need to get downstairs. And mom should be here any time now."

I step out of the doorway, "After you."

Natasha flows down the hall and the stairs like a queen and I am so proud of my friend. I release the front of the barrier, reshaping things to prevent anyone from wandering in from the back yard or going around from the

front yard to enter through the backdoor. I have to keep the
shield up anyway so that the smoke will be concealed and
I can filter it to keep it concealed. I cast an illusion over
the barrier so that everything will continue to look as it
does now. The death witches arrive and the mourners do
to, along with the opportunists. I see Natasha's mother go
upstairs and return downstairs with the jewelry box,
heading directly for her car. I wave at the bodyguards to
ignore it and they do. Billy notices and he makes certain
that Natasha does not, yet. I meet his eye and he shakes his
head sadly. We both know she is going to be heartbroken,
but not today if we can help it.

The rest of the afternoon goes quickly. Natasha lights
the funeral pyre and accelerates the flames, I keep everything well filtered and our security detail stays busy. John
found a gnome attempting to crawl inside a cupboard to
hide. He quietly escorted him out and told him that if he
came back in he would be on the menu. The food was
plentiful and Maria set it out like she created the banquet
herself. I swear she is part kitchen witch. People trickled
out while others wandered in. Everyone paid their respects
to Natasha, her mother left shortly after the pyre was lit,
saying the smell gave her a headache. Everyone with extra
sensitive sensory perception looked sharp at her when she
said that, but she was oblivious. Natasha's father never
showed up. I don't know if her mother even noticed how
everyone cleared the way for her to leave and conversa-
tions died as she drew near.

By nightfall the last stragglers were gone. Memré was

still angry with Natasha's mom and the others that had attempted to do similar things. But so were we all. It was Memré, after she arrived, that made sure Natasha never saw the others, she guided Natasha so skillfully that sometimes it took Billy a second to figure out why she was distracting her. I think Natasha realized by nightfall what was going on but she just smiled sadly and hugged Memré.

Once everything is cleaned up we all leave the house and let Natasha walk through one more time with Billy and Memré. Memré was all set to excuse herself when Natasha asked her to stay. We wait in silence until they join us outside. I close the barrier around the entire house, turning it into a sphere, while it doesn't disturb the ground, it does go through it. Anyone trying to dig under it will be upset, it is a closed sphere.

The ride home is happily uneventful. We are all just getting into the house when Natasha's mother starts blowing up her phone. Three texts arrive and then it immediately starts ringing. Billy gently takes the phone from her, reads the texts, and silences her phone. He sets it on the table in the entry and taking Natasha's hand he walks with her to their bedroom. I don't have to read the messages to know it was nothing good, Billy's face said it all. For tonight, we are going to let it be. The shields are up here and there, Natasha's mom isn't getting through tonight and neither is anyone else.

Eighteen

FATE

AFTER ALL THE drama of today I am just glad to be home. I walk up the stairs with Charles on one side and Devon on the other. I don't want to choose who sleeps in my bed tonight. I want the comfort of both of them and I really want the grounding that the sex would bring. I actually would like to have them both. I know as a vampire my body was capable of doing and accepting more than I could as a human and I feel like that is probably the case with being a goddess. I want to test the theory.

They have to be ok with that too for it to happen. We get to my door and I step forward, turning to face them. "I would really like to have you both with me tonight. I understand if you are not agreeable to that, but tonight I am not choosing. So, you two flip a coin or whatever you need to do to decide if only one of you will be coming in.

While you are at that, I am going to enter my bedroom and get naked and crawl into the bed. Try not to keep me waiting too long."

That said I open the door to my sitting room and leaving that open I walk across to my bedroom door, opening the double doors to enter and then turning to close them behind me. I smile at them standing in the sitting room doorway as I close the bedroom doors. I can hear them speaking to each other but I choose not to tune in, it isn't my business. I shed shoes and clothes as I walk across the room to my bed. I get one leg up on the bed when the door opens. The two of them are standing there and Charles says, "Don't move. Stay right where you are now."

I raise an eyebrow but hold still as he whispers to Devon. Devon grins and strolls over. He kicks off his shoes and runs his fingers lightly down my back. Charles enters the room, shutting the door behind him as Devon takes his hands off me. I hear him moving behind me as I watch Charles take off his tie. He drops it as he walks across the room. He slips off his jacket and Devon's tongue slips into my core. I moan at the shock and pleasure of it as he pays attention to every inch of my pussy with his eager lips and tongue. When my eyes open again Charles is shirtless and unbuttoning his pants. My breathing is ragged as Devon slips two fingers into me and focuses the efforts of lips and tongue on my clit. Charles is gloriously naked when my eyes open again, he gets on the bed across from me and crawls over to me, on his knees in front of me he slips a hand in my hair, gripping it hard. He kisses me harder, his tongue invading my mouth and I love it. Below me Devon hits my g-spot with his fingers while his tongue does magic on my clit and I cum all over his face, my legs shaking and the kiss broken as my entire body convulses and I light up the room.

Devon and Charles save me from hitting the floor, Devon grabbing the leg holding me up and bracing it while Charles grabs an arm with his free hand. I gasp, "Wait, pause for a minute. At least till I can support my self again." Devon gives my clit one last mind blowing kiss and I feel him moving around behind me again.My breathing calms and Charles starts kissing my neck, trailing kisses down one side and then moving to the other. He bites me and sips from my neck, I tip my head and the leg that was on the bed slips to the floor so I can stretch to press into the bite. Devon steps up behind me and I feel him press into me, stretching the walls of my pussy in the most delicious way. I feel his hips touch my skin, he holds there for the briefest moment before he pulls nearly all the way out just as slowly. I could cry in frustration but then he slams in, over and over. I can feel the wave of another orgasm building as Charles releases my neck to trail kisses down my chest and suck a nipple into his mouth, biting it hard enough to make me gasp and then kissing its puck-ered tip gently as his hand trails down my belly to slip two fingers between my lips and rub slow circles on my clit while his mouth moves to pay attention to my other breast. Devon starts moving faster and I am nearly there with him, thrusts in as far as he can go one last time, his hands gripping my hips as he yells my name. I am so close but Charles moved his fingers away just before Devon came. I whimper with the need, Charles sits back on his ankles, "Ready for a ride Goddess?"

Devon chuckles as he pulls out of me. He slaps my ass and growls, "Get up there."

I turn and grin at him. Then looking back at Charles I push him onto his back as I climb on he bed and over him. Positioning myself over him I press my lips onto the head of his cock, everything is so slick my lips part for his swollen head and I melt around his cock as I lower myself onto him. I rotate my hips while sitting with him fully buried within me and he moans, grabbing my legs. Seeing the effect it has on him I roll my hips as I lift up and then slam down. I get a rhythm going, rolling my hips on the upswing and then slam down, his moans are fuel to the fire, then Devon whispers in my ear, "Turn around." I roll my hips all the way up and off Charles' cock, making him whimper this time, and I reposition myself to reverse cowgirl.

As I lower myself onto him he grabs my ass in both hands, "I have always loved your ass."

Devon is sitting on his knees in front of me and he leans forward, but instead of kissing me he heads straight for my breasts. Kissing and stroking them as I ride Charles. I can feel Charles is nearly there and I stop rotating my hips, leaning into Devon's face I brace myself with my hands on the bed, Charles hands gripping my hips and pushing me up and down faster and faster till we both explode into the stars. I feel something warm on my breasts and realize Devon has cum too. I grin at him and give him a kiss. He still has the sweetest kisses I have ever tasted. We rest in place for a few minutes before we decide that perhaps a shower is in order to wash all this off.

I have never showered with two men, the experience is not a bad one. They washed my entire body and I came twice more.

I don't know what the future holds for me beyond really great sex with two gorgeous men. For tonight, I will pretend it is nothing more than them and trying to do as much good in this world as I possibly can.

The problems that Pru and Demeter and whoever this Beast is will bring are worries for another day. Right now, I am pleasantly tired, happily sated and whatever comes tomorrow I will face it and I will keep my family safe.

***

Author's Note

Reviews really help other people decide whether or not to read a book. If you feel a way about this book, I would sincerely appreciate a review.

About the Author

Rhiannon writes steamy paranormal romance. She is an avid reader of many authors in a variety of genre though she tends more toward paranormal.

She has three former pound puppies that she dotes on and three daughters that she adores.

Rhiannon has lived in multiple states though she is currently residing in North Carolina. Wandering, witching, and reading with her puppies and husband are what she does when she isn't writing.

To learn about what is happening in Rhiannon's world and get loads of pupper cuteness, sign up for the by using the QR code below to visit my website.

Also by Rhiannon Futch

The Daughter of the Moon series-

<u>Selena Rose, Daughter of the Moon Book 1</u>

<u>Thorns of the Rose, Daughter of the Moon Book 2</u>

<u>Heart of the Rose, Daughter of the Moon Book 3</u>

The Fate's Chronicles series

<u>A Vampire's Fate</u>

<u>A Vampire's Treasure</u>

<u>A Vampire's Dream</u>

<u>A Vampire's Chase</u>

<u>A Vampire's Fight</u>

<u>Fated for Halloween -</u> only available via email signup

The Belancore Witches of North Carolina series

<u>Witchy Ever After</u>

<u>A Witchy New Year</u>

<u>My Witchy Valentine</u>

Sin series

<u>Sin on a Dark Knight</u>

<u>Sin on a Broken Heart</u>

<u>Sin on a Burning Heart</u>

Sin on a Vengeful Heart

The Vampire Kings Series

Mercy of the Vampire King

Shame of the Vampire King

Pursuit of the Vampire King

Prey of the Vampire King

Reign of the Vampire King

Coming Soon

Love and Vampires Series

Olivia's Fall

Olivia's Prison

Olivia's Flight

Olivia's Family

Warriors of the Old Gods

A Dream of Blood

A Dream of Wolves

A Dream of Stone

A Dream of Ravens

A Dream of Bones